SALVAGE MARINES
NECROSPACE BOOK 1

SEAN-MICHAEL ARGO

SEVERED PRESS
HOBART TASMANIA

SALVAGE MARINES

TABLE OF CONTENTS

PROLOGUE

It is the Age of The Corporation.

The common man toils under the watchful eye of the elite and their enforcers. The rules of law have long been replaced by the politics of profit. For many centuries, the Covenants of Commerce have ruled mankind, from boardroom to factory floor, from mine deep to fertile field, upon the battlefields of heart, of mind, and of distant star.

The dark ages of feudalism have returned with capitalistic ferocity. There is no peace among the stars of mapped space; business is booming.

Impoverished workers drown in debt, laboring for subsistence pay. Mercenaries of every kind wage war, loyal to the banner of any company willing to meet their price. Everyone in existence is locked in a ceaseless struggle for economic dominance and survival. Scavengers and space pirates swoop in to loot what they can from the forgotten and unprotected.

To be a human being in such times is to be one among countless billions in a civilization spread across a vast universe, all ensnared in the same blood-soaked web of capitalism, most doomed to be ground to dust amidst the gears of progress.

There are some people, however, those rare few, who rise from the ranks of the faceless masses, to make their mark upon history.

This is one such tale.

DEATH AND TAXES

Samuel Hyst had been standing in line for nearly four hours, just behind his lifelong friend Ben Takeda. Both young men silently and grimly waited their turn to speak with the graduation administrator.

Now eighteen standard years of age and despite his academic scores being rather average, he had qualified for graduation. He was thankful for it. No one wanted to remain in the Citizen Academy for any longer than they absolutely had to.

Though he had few aspirations beyond graduation, he was positive that accruing more debt while he figured out those aspirations was not the most prudent choice. Each year spent in academy added another year of debt servitude for the average citizen who would, at best, go on to earn an average wage.

Samuel did, however, have a penchant for curiosity, and he often felt he was missing something in life, craving it even, though he couldn't figure out exactly what it was that he sought. Like so many others in his age group, Samuel had been raised completely within the public system provided by Grotto Corporation, the company that was the ruling body of his world.

Samuel Hyst had been born on Baen 6, one of the eleven planets in the Baen System, which was owned and operated by the galaxy spanning mega-corporation known as Grotto.

Every other planet in the Baen system was simply named Baen, with a numerical modifier, the company obviously being more interested in efficiency than imagination when it came to the naming of planets.

The same held true for the names of people, machines, and many other elements of Grotto society. The primary business interest of Grotto Corporation was the exploitation of raw materials, ranging from gases, minerals, metals, or in Samuel's case, human resources.

Due to the company's focus on the base materials of industry, Grotto was one of the largest and most wealthy of the trade empires. It was also one of the most grindingly brutal with regards to its citizenry.

The masters of the corporation had created a debt-based society in which the citizens were charged by the corporation for compulsory education, health care, and housing requirements.

Citizens graduated from their compulsory education with anywhere from fifteen to eighteen years of accrued debt already logged against their credit lines. Including the costs of housing, health care and the everyday expense of being alive, resulted in subsistence level living conditions for the majority of the population as they labored for the company trying to pay off debt that would always outpace their wages.

People reached retirement age with little or nothing to pass on to their children except their own remaining debt, resulting in their offspring inheriting old debt from family members while accruing new debts of their own. These institutionalized debts were known as life-bonds.

In front of Samuel, Ben shifted impatiently. Always somewhat of a malcontent, he consistently found himself in trouble with academy authorities as a result of his inability to keep his mouth shut about any and everything that bothered him.

"You know there are elite families that exist at the top of this whole mess who inherit money, reserved spots at university and trade schools, even whole factories and planets, man," Ben whispered harshly over his shoulder towards Samuel as the two of them waited for their turn with the administrator. "What kind of jobs are going to be left for normal folks like us if we can't even get enough of a credit line after academy to buy training?"

Samuel nodded in agreement, partly out of habit, as it was the only way to get Ben to quiet down, but also because he actually did agree with his friend. While there were many trade empires in the universe that ruled their populations through debt-servitude, Grotto was unique in that the ruling class elites were also the skilled working class of Grotto society. Granted access by their extreme wealth to the expensive post-academy education, many of the elites of Grotto were trained in industrial trades and took a fierce pride in that fact.

"It's like this bloodline workforce system keeps the low born down and the high born up," grumbled Ben, whose demeanor had been growing increasingly sour the closer he got to the administrator, as if the eventual and inevitable fate of having his life-bond sealed was pushing him to new heights of philosophical fury. "If we can't get trained for any jobs with wages that can get us out of the life-bond, then how are we going to get our kids into training either? It's like I'm still a damn teenager and I already know that my kids are going to end up just like me. We're trapped, man. Even your dad, I know he taught himself all that metalwork, but since it's not accredited he still can't get high wage work."

"Ben, just take a deep breath and let's get through today, we'll worry about social injustice tomorrow, okay?" Samuel placed a reassuring hand on his friend's shoulder, "And you're wrong about my dad, he did some off-book fabrication for the forge steward at Assemblage 23 last month."

"Seriously? What kind of credits did he pull?" asked Ben with an astonished, even if slightly admonishing, expression on his face.

"No money, just favors. Dad got him to set me up with a Tier 3 position on the line. It would have taken me something like five years to get a gig like that on my own." He and Ben both saw that the person in front of them was finished and it was now Ben's turn, "I promise you, buddy," Samuel said, "if I ever get a chance to pay it forward, you know I've got your back. Like I said, let's just get through today."

Ben set his jaw and nodded grimly, then stepped into the booth of the graduation administrator. Samuel couldn't hear what was being said on the other side of the sliding booth door, so he looked around the building to see how the rest of the lines were doing.

The domed building had been temporarily re-purposed for the graduation ceremony of Academy 427 and already nearly two thousand graduates had been processed.

Something slamming into the sliding door of the booth in front of him drew Samuel's attention back to the line just before he was shouldered aside by a large man wearing riot armor.

The man was one of the proctors, the guards who maintained crowd control during graduation ceremonies and on the streets of Baen in general. Samuel had heard that sometimes graduation day was rough. There was something profoundly upsetting about the actuality of having the life-bond presented to you that weighed heavier on young people than the mere concept of it.

As the door opened, Samuel could see that Ben had bloodied the administrator's nose and was screaming at him. In short order the proctor jabbed Ben with an electrified baton and the youth collapsed in a heap.

Samuel cursed under his breath, knowing that several nights in the youth detention center was only going to put a negative mark on Ben's life-bond, which would make him even more undesirable to the various labor chiefs.

Inside, the administrator dabbed at his nose while another proctor arrived and the two men hauled out Ben's unconscious body.

Samuel swallowed with nervousness and stepped inside as the administrator impatiently waved him in. Samuel followed the administrator's silent invitation to sit down, and then the sliding door closed behind him.

"Samuel Hyst, son of Saul and Marion Hyst," said the administrator, more to himself than Samuel it seemed, as he thumbed through the files on a handheld data-pad. "Let's see what we have on you." He murmured to himself as he read. "No inherited debts, as of yet. Both parents still living, median test scores. Ah yes, here we are, aptitude assessment scores."

Samuel blinked in surprise. "I'm sorry sir, when did we take aptitude tests? I don't remember that exam." He leaned forward in a half-attempt to read the administrator's screen.

"Oh, it's not a single exam, young man. Data for the assessment is gathered from your first day in academy onwards, with additional data points coming from your family history, hab-block of birth, and medical records," stated the administrator matter-of-factly as he scrolled through the arcane graphs and charts presented on his screen. "This information will inform us as to what your career options are within the Grotto workforce, which as you know is requisite to paying back your life-bond."

"I've been thinking that I'd like to-," Samuel started to say before the administrator cut him off sharply.

"Desire is irrelevant, young man. If desire dictated a person's place in the workforce then the forges would grow cold, the lights would go dark, and the human race would go back to living in caves. Now, drop the questions and let me do my job," spat the administrator as he pulled a second screen from his desk and flipped it around so that Samuel could see. "According to the assessments, you are an ideal candidate for waste disposal, janitorial, and food service. All three of those are our largest labor sectors, so we should have no problem placing your life-bond with a suitable labor chief."

"What about working the line? My father is in the forge at Assemblage 23, he was told there would be a place for me there," protested Samuel, who almost got out of his seat before remembering that there were likely proctors watching this particular booth after Ben's outburst.

"Regardless of what opportunities may or may not exist at Assemblage 23, and that is conjecture, your life-bond is due today, and forge work was not an appropriate match for the data present in your aptitude assessment." The administrator produced a hypo dispenser and held his open hand out, "Now, give me your hand and let's get this life-bond administered."

"That's it? You just look at some data and decide my life?" grumbled Samuel. "No wonder Ben punched you in the face." He held his hand out to the administrator.

The administrator stabbed Samuel's wrist with the hypo and the needle deposited a small microchip in the young man's wrist. Samuel already knew that the chip contained the sum total of his digital information, his academy scores, his medical records, his total Grotto debts, and now, his workforce assessment. Knowing about it, and seeing it, were very different, and he found himself deeply troubled in a way that he had not expected.

Grotto life was hard, and often disappointing, but his father had taught him to try do his best, to live today for today. As Samuel sat back and rubbed his wrist it seemed like a hollow piece of advice, like something a person would say to themselves if they were afraid to look past the boundaries of today and see that all the tomorrows would never change.

"Samuel, I understand that you may feel that you have more to offer Grotto than what exists within the limitations of your workforce assessment," the administrator offered, his expression softening somewhat, "My advice is take the job you can get, and work hard, give yourself a chance to settle into a routine."

Then the administrator opened a sliding drawer and handed Samuel a small digi-card. It was colored blue, and simply had the word REAPER stamped on one side. He knew that the card would activate and display whatever message or data that was stored within once he slotted it into a data-pad or wall terminal, though he wasn't sure what it was for.

"What is REAPER?" he asked as the administrator stood up and gestured for Samuel to leave.

"The only job for which the aptitude assessment is irrelevant. If you find yourself unable to cope with your new life, much like that boy who assaulted me, then activate that card," he said as the door opened and he gently pushed Samuel out so that the next person in line could enter, "Risk and reward young man, consider it an alternative to crime or suicide."

It had been two long years since the graduation administrator had given Samuel the REAPER card, and though he still kept it, the young man had only activated it once. After what he had learned, Samuel had placed it high on a shelf in his room and did his best to forget it.

At the time, he had been struggling with disappointment over his workforce assignment. Not only had his father done fabrication work in exchange for a favor he could not call in, but because of Samuel's limited workforce prospects, there was little hope of him paying off his life-bond, much less affording any schooling to better his situation.

Samuel had begrudgingly taken work in the food service sector. He spent most of his ten-hour shifts on an assembly line preparing and packaging bland meals of protein blocks, fiber sticks, and nutrient powder. Once the meals had been prepared, packaged, and crated, they were distributed by a fleet of transport skiffs to the various forges, factories, and refineries that covered the surface of Baen 6.

Samuel had no clear idea where the food came from-- likely some agri-world outside the otherwise harsh environment of the Baen system-- only that his plant removed bulk ingredients from off-world shipments and processed them for Baen workforce consumption.

Most Grotto labor sectors included a meal plan, which of course was compulsory and automatically deducted from each worker's pay, regardless of whether or not they ate the meals. As a result, Samuel's plant ran day and night to match the demand for calories from the planet's workforce.

At least the work was easy, Samuel had managed to tell himself, even if monotonous. He had told himself this many times and he had managed to find a modicum of peace in it.

The pay for assembly line work was low, but since he was not rated for any other work, he was forced to make ends meet as best he could. For the first year, Samuel lived with his mother and father, as did most graduates for at least the first few years, assuming they ever accumulated enough to move out on their own. Samuel saved enough in housing payments that when he met Sura Kameni he was able to make the decision to move out on his own.

She was from a different Hab-Block and though most people did not venture out of their own districts, she had decided on a whim to explore. Sura had simply boarded the metro and decided to get off at the first stop that looked interesting. She was a photographic artist, which was something Samuel had never heard of until she asked for permission to take his photo.

Samuel had been sitting on the concrete steps of the district's Spire, which was a skyscraper that housed the local police force and public surveillance operations. He was waiting for Ben Takeda to be released from jail. Again.

Ben had been jailed for nearly a week, without pay, for brawling with a site foreman at the sewage processing plant where he'd been assigned. This was Ben's second offense that year. It had been nearly twelve months since his assault on the graduation administrator. A third workforce related incident would result in a penal reclassification and he would be shipped to one of the mining compounds that clung to the various moons and asteroids that filled the Baen system.

Something about Samuel's posture as he waited for his friend had struck Sura as indicative of life in Grotto as a whole, and she needed to capture it. At first, she snapped several photos before approaching him, and then the troubled young man had agreed to remain and allow her more photos.

"I don't have a license for it, so no quality control division or public surveillance office is going to hire me to gallivant around the Baen system," she had said, brazenly snapping away at Samuel as he sat on the concrete steps of a Grotto executive office spire, "But I just love doing it, so when I'm off shift I just travel wherever the metro takes me and shoot what's interesting."

"What do you do with your photos after you take them?" Samuel had asked incredulously as he did his best not to stare at her. She was easily the most attractive woman who had ever spoken to him. "I've never seen anyone take photos for no reason."

"There's plenty of reasons. To see things in a different way, maybe show people something new." She had laughed easily as she snapped a few more before sitting down next to Samuel and showing him some of the photos in her digital display, "Have you ever seen yourself? Like through someone else's eyes?"

"I'm nobody special, why would it matter?" Samuel asked, trying to follow her logic, until she came upon a particularly stark photo of him that she had taken before speaking to him. Samuel was taken aback at how haggard he looked. With the hard edges of the Spire in the background, and her black and white filter, it was a grim image.

"I see a man who knows that the universe is a hard place, that life under Grotto Corporation is a heavy thing," Sura said as she showed him the photo, seemingly so caught up in the shot that she didn't notice as Samuel looked at her, "But he strives to carry on. There's power in that."

Samuel looked at himself in the mirror of the tiny wash unit that occupied a corner of the bar he had asked Ben to meet him at for a drink. Two years on the assembly line and to his eyes he looked far older than twenty.

There was a toll being paid by his body and mind, he thought to himself, and it wasn't until now that he realized just how telling that photo Sura had taken really was.

He and Sura had continued talking, and over the next few weeks found themselves enjoying each other's company more and more as their budding friendship transformed into more.

Sura saw the world so differently from Samuel, and he felt as if she was a sun around which he was an orbiting planet. Sura also worked in food service, though she often had to push for re-assignment due to unwanted attention from co-workers or site foremen and she always teetered on the edge of financial ruin as a result.

Samuel was their foundation, and though they often found themselves having to make hard choices about their life-style, they managed to be as happy as a Grotto couple could be. She often told him that she thought it no accident that they found each other among the swell of humanity, and together, they strived to make the best of their lot in life. They had lived like that for just over a year, until last week.

Sura was pregnant.

Samuel walked back to his table, where Ben sat nursing a beverage so day-glow green it looked radioactive. The other man had a similar weary look despite his young age, understandably so, since Ben had been working in waste disposal.

It was a grueling, physical job, and since Grotto Corporation had determined that manual labor was a cheaper alternative to high-end machinery, whenever possible, assembly lines, factories, and in Ben's case, waste disposal, used hard physical labor in place of machines.

Ben had echoed Samuel's father in his frustrated indictment that Grotto had intentionally regressed and eschewed technological advancement in favor of further expanding the Great and Holy Bottom Line.

"So what did you want to talk about, man?" asked Ben as Samuel sat down and took a furtive sip from his own glass. "I know you only drink like, once every hundred years, so I figure whatever you've got to say it's big."

"Do you remember that REAPER card?" Samuel said after knocking back his entire drink and gesturing to the waitress for a second round. "It's been on my mind lately."

"Brother, you invite me out to a bar, which you never do, you get three drinks in before saying anything other than small talk and then you open with that?" laughed Ben as he took a swig of his drink, "Seems like you've been thinking real hard about it."

"Sura is pregnant," Samuel stated, then paused as Ben took another swallow while the waitress brought Samuel's refill.

They sat in grim silence for a full minute before Ben finally spoke, "You're going to do it, aren't you?"

"It's already done," stated Samuel as he took a strong pull from his drink, "I signed the contract this morning."

"Whoa, man! Hold on a minute. Does Sura know? Did she see this coming?" sputtered Ben, baffled at his friend's casual delivery of such grave news.

"The physician confirmed it two days ago, we're having a boy," rasped Samuel, as if Ben hadn't spoken, his voice choking up with emotion as his eyes began to moisten, "His name is going to be Orion."

"I mean, congratulations brother, but seriously, Sura has no idea what you've signed on for? What you've signed *her* on for?" Ben asked.

"She won't like it, but she'll come around. You've said it yourself a thousand times, Ben, we're born into a life we can't escape from, just like our parents. If I don't do something to change that, then Orion is going to end up just like me," Samuel growled in frustration, the edge of his voice hardened by the alcohol. "You were right to punch that son of a bitch at graduation. This was a raw deal from the start."

"So why are you telling me and not Sura right now, huh?" Ben retorted just before draining his glass and gesturing to the waitress for another.

"The recruiter said that Baen system is one week away from a new fleet founding. If you sign on now, we'd end up in the same unit," Samuel said, his gaze downcast and his foot tapping nervously on the floor. "I didn't want to tell Sura until I could also tell her that you had my back. She's always thought the world of you."

"I'm one fist fight away from a penal colony, not sure what she sees in me," Ben laughed.

"That's my point. You don't back down. That makes you a crappy janitor," Samuel insisted, "but I bet that would make you a hell of a soldier."

"Now you sound like a recruiter," Ben growled as he accepted the new drink from the waitress and sucked down half of it in one strong pull. "There a signing bonus if you get me to come with?"

"This is Grotto, of course there's a bonus for convincing your friends to sign on the dotted line," snorted Samuel as he finished his drink, "Look, just think about it. Being line workers and shit shovelers on Baen 6 is no kind of life, not for us, and not for our families. We could do this, and make something better for ourselves."

Samuel finished his drink and set a disposable credit stick on the table to cover the tab. He patted Ben's shoulder and left the bar.

Ben sat alone for quite some time, saying nothing. Eventually, he finished his drink and pulled a brand new REAPER card from his jacket pocket, turning it over and over in his hands before slotting it into his handheld data-pad.

REAPER– Resource Exploration And Procurement Engineer Regiment

Welcome Citizen, to a new life of adventure, including meal plan and hazard pay!

Because Grotto Corporation is heavily invested in exploration and military ventures there is always a place for stalwart citizens, twenty-five standard years or younger, willing to risk life and limb for incredible wages and a sense of accomplishment.

As a REAPER, your primary function will be to serve as foot soldiers and salvage specialists for militarized expeditions into regions of both mapped and unmapped space in search of raw materials ready to be exploited. To claim or re-claim machinery, equipment, and building materials from former battlefields, space hulks, and otherwise abandoned facilities.

Base wages for training and transit time are nearly twice that of the average workforce assignment, and all recovery and combat duties come with additional hazard bonuses.

See your local recruiter for details.

Sign up today!

Ben took a deep breath and put the data-pad and card back in his jacket, then left the bar to walk into the evening streets.

MINING UNIT 5597

Basic had been hard on Samuel, as it was on every new recruit, though particularly so for the young man who had just put everything on the line for his budding family. Or at least that's what Samuel continued to tell himself as he fought his way through the sweaty grind of physical training, the scorching heat of the salvage tool orientations, and the concussive repetition of firearms assessment and operations.

In truth, it felt somewhat like a defeat, as if he'd retreated from an unhappy life and a dismal future rather than taking an opportunity to carve out a better one. It felt selfish, and though Sura had spoken only words of encouragement and support, Samuel could see disappointment in her eyes and could sense a growing distance between them as she constructed emotional walls to protect herself. Just as Samuel trained his body for war, so did Sura harden her heart for the long haul on the home front.

Samuel knew enough about himself to know that he was more of the 'strong, silent type' when it came to matters of the heart and part of his personal quest during basic REAPER training was to become a better communicator. In the end, communication was all that he and Sura had left.

In the last few days of training he had been informed that the newly founded Baen REAPER fleet had already been issued marching orders. There would be no time to see their families or have shore leave. Basic training was to continue to its conclusion on board the massive tug ship that would serve as both home and base of operations for the Reapers.

Samuel and Sura were allowed video streams and audio contact as each marine quarters came equipped with a com-deck, and the spouses did the best they could through the mediums available.

It wasn't much, but it was something.

Samuel looked ahead at his friend Ben Takeda and smiled inside his helmet. The few months between their conversation in the bar and now being deployed on their first mission had been hard, but Ben had helped Samuel through it all.

Ben had found that he was indeed well suited to the life of a soldier and showed an early aptitude for the heavy machine gun. Samuel often thought that it was the positive shift of Ben's newfound zest for life as a REAPER that helped Samuel keep himself together.

During basic training the entry level REAPER pay rate was not only more money than either man had ever earned before, it was more than either of their parents had ever made.

Ben had run the numbers and discovered that with the base rate he would be able to clear his life-bond within five years. Ben insisted that after five years as a REAPER he had little intention of going back to being a Grotto civilian. Working for Grotto, he would still be on the waste disposal detail, so for him at least, the plan was REAPER until death or retirement.

As Samuel met other new recruits in basic, the exotic beauty, Jada Sek, and the exceptionally average, Spencer Green, for example, he discovered that Ben's attitude was common. Samuel had little desire to be a soldier for the rest of his life, though when he calculated the life-bonds for both he and Sura on top of the expatriation fee, he was going to have to survive nearly a decade of service.

For Samuel and all of the rest of the recruits, the real game changer was the hazard pay bonuses. If a REAPER spent even just half a standard year officially "deployed" on an operation, whether it was combat or salvage or both, the pay was nearly double the standard rate.

Samuel had never wanted war, though when he compared five years of deployed hazard time to ten years of basic service to accomplish his goals and get his family away from Grotto, he found himself very willing to take up arms. So long as the paychecks kept clearing he would keep fighting.

It was this vision of his future life and future family that kept him warm in the cold of space, and though he knew it was just as much of a daydream as anything else, he clung to it. There was strength in his goals, a purpose beyond himself that he hoped would push him to excel in combat and to survive whatever the universe had in store for him.

So it was that Samuel and Ben were rolled into Tango Platoon, along with orphans Patrick Baen and Aaron Baen. Their squad leader position, known as Boss, was filled by Maggie Taggart. The marines called her Boss Taggart to her face, but thought of her as Mag when they weren't addressing her.

Mag was a tough-as-nails veteran, as was Boss Lucinda Ulanti and Boss Wynn Marsters, assigned from other Reaper fleets to be leaders for the Baen 6 founding fleet. It was these veterans who set the standard for what it meant to be a REAPER.

It was they who would not only lead the marines, but also teach them through action, how to take what the new recruits had learned in basic and execute it in the field.

Samuel's grip tightened on his combat rifle as he looked behind him once more into the darkness of the tunnel, silently hoping that the training had been enough.

"Everybody watch your corners, just because someone already swept it doesn't mean something hasn't show up in the meantime," Mag growled into her com-bead as she raised her combat rifle to point the muzzle into the darkness of the corridor in front of her. The mounted light on the rifle illuminated a small bend on the right that indicated a side passage. "We don't want to get flanked if there really is something in here with us."

"Copy that, Boss," said Samuel in a low voice, partly through the com-bead and partly to himself, as he'd certainly not double checked either of the last two passages they'd come through since entering the labyrinth of corridors that made up the underbelly of the compound.

His imagination threatened to conjure up any number of horrors from childhood stories, and he retreated into his firearm routine to calm his nerves.

Ever since basic, he habitually checked the safety of his weapon, and then looked at the ammunition read out on the side of the gun. He had not fired a single shot outside of training, and certainly not twenty minutes into his first salvage mission, but the young man took an obsessive comfort in the assurance that he had control of his weapon and a full magazine.

The fleet had set anchor in low orbit around a small planet with no name beyond designation M5597. In the pre-drop briefing the shift manager had informed the marines that fourteen years prior, a mining branch ship was sent to this planet in response to data returned by unmanned probes revealing large deposits of biridium and mordite gases. As both resources were labor intensive and time-consuming to extract, a ship outfitted with the ability to found a mining compound was dispatched. After several years of acceptable levels of production yields, communication with M5597 abruptly ceased.

The entire 5500 sector was considered low security space, so keeping military vessels in the area was deemed unnecessary. The transport way station, after missing two consecutive deliveries, had filed an automatic report.

Once the regional managers of the sector, who worked out of the Home Office on Grotto Prime, were made aware of the report they determined that the cost of a response effort would outweigh the projected profits of the facility.

At the time, Grotto Corp. was engaged in a bitter trade war with the Hadrian Conglomerate in several of the surrounding sectors. To re-task even one response ship to pass through the war zone and into sector 5500 would have not only resulted in the loss of the ship to one or more of the many Hadrian frigates that picketed the area, but also ran the risk of Hadrian management discovering that there were precious resources hidden on a small planet deep within the largely ignored and unmapped sector.

The report was buried and the fate of the mining compound on M5597 was unknown.

It had been ten standard years since then and the war with Hadrian had eventually ground to a halt as more lucrative ventures had presented themselves to both companies in other parts of the universe.

Two weeks ago the branch ship that had sourced the mining compound, which should have been the ship to deliver the production yields all those years ago, had been sighted several systems away and flagged as a rogue ship, no doubt being crewed by pirates or independents.

The companies that dominated the universe, though in constant conflict with one another, did ostensibly share information about independents and pirates, as both groups represented a challenge to corporate rule.

Once flagged as a rogue vessel the ship would be 'red listed' alongside thousands of others. They simply ceased to exist as far as being under the protection or responsibility of any company. While this certainly represented a kind of freedom, Red Listed ships, and static communities for that matter, were completely on their own. They had no allegiance to anyone, which meant they also had no rights. Most Red Listed ships and communities quickly turned to piracy in order to survive, were wiped out by a corporate interest, or were simply swallowed by the void of space and never heard from again.

A new regional manager on Grotto Prime, so far removed from the field that even the shift manager did not have their name in her briefing, had decided to classify M5597 as a REAPER objective.

Samuel had listened attentively, not once flinching at the shameless bureaucracy and adherence to the bottom line that ruled Grotto society. He had long ago accepted that such things were unchanging. It made perfect sense to him that the managers, both old and new, made their decisions based on the profit and loss projections of their actions. Such was the Grotto way, and he had been raised in that world, as had the other hundred and forty marines.

It was the logical choice now that the trade war was over and there was a new regional manager looking to boost his or her quarterly revenues and political status within the organization.

Sending a REAPER fleet was relatively inexpensive, and since the cost of the entire facility had already been tagged as a loss, any salvage or resource yield would be pure profit. The shift manager went on to say that, as per standard operational procedures, the marines were to do their best to avoid further damaging the compound should they be met with armed resistance.

It was that thought of armed resistance that hurled Samuel's mind back into the present moment and he once more checked his safety and ammunition count.

Squad Taggart had made planetfall roughly twenty minutes prior and though their drop-pods were out-dated and uncomfortable, they were sturdy. As they'd been coming down, Samuel had found himself looking at the blast scarring on the interior of the pod, and realized that at some point in this pod's history an incendiary device had gone off inside it. He hoped that the marines within had already exited the craft since salvage marines weren't usually dropped into direct combat, though it was anybody's guess what had happened.

Record keeping was more concerned with resources expended and resources procured and there was little in the way of storytelling amongst the marines. They were a grim lot, being the lowest paid and most poorly equipped of the Grotto military even though they were always being sent into the unknown.

As Samuel swept his rifle through the gloom of the corridor he found himself wondering if it might have been better to be a legionnaire. At least then he would have bio-implants to make him faster and stronger, an armored dropsuit, and access to the most impressive and deadly of armaments. However, he told himself, instead of prowling the dark corridors of mysteriously abandoned mining facilities in the middle of necrospace he would be in the middle of a firefight with enemy soldiers who were just as powerful as he was. Samuel was a pragmatic young man, and had been raised Grotto from birth, so as the seconds ticked by he considered that his pay-per-minute as a marine was the better choice for a family man.

A sharp scream that could not have been human filled the corridors, and Samuel's blood felt like it had turned to ice. Suddenly the unknown of an alien threat seemed much more intimidating than fighting other humans.

Samuel had always heard stories and rumors of inhuman creatures that stalked the forgotten corners of space, and there were always tales of ancient aliens who ruled the frontiers of necrospace. Like most people, he had ignored them, though in that moment, there was no doubt in his mind that monsters were real and that one was inside the dark compound with them.

"Tighten up people, this is what you've been training for," muttered Mag as she held a fist up for the squad to stop, "This is a big place, sounds like that could carry serious distance, whatever it is could be on the other side of the compound for all we know. Aaron what's our position?"

"The rig says we're only about two hundred meters from the central quarters, Boss," said Aaron as he checked the data-deck affixed to his forearm which contained all of their mission specifics, including maps of the facility and last known inventory lists. "Could be that whatever it is came in through the tunnels on the far side of the compound."

"Squad Ulanti entered on that side. With all the atmospheric interference we aren't going to hear anything from them until we're face to face," grumbled Mag as she lifted her rifle and continued forward, "Keep it together, people, let's breach the compound and get out of these freaking tunnels."

The squad began to move forward again and Samuel, who was bringing up the rear, could not help but turn to peer down the corridor behind them. He was astounded that the three other marines, raw recruits just like him, seemed so unshaken by the scream. Mag, as a Reaper veteran of at least ten years, he could understand, but the certain knowledge that something was in here with them, something not human, had rattled him to the core.

Suddenly, the combat rifle in his hands provided less assurance than it had moments before and checking the ammunition read out did little to steady his mind. He stood there, looking into the darkness and could almost swear that he could see shapes moving in the black. The illumination from his mounted light seemed to be swallowed by the pitch darkness of the corridors and just beyond the edges of his sight he felt a menacing presence.

"Hyst, snap out of it, man," said Ben, as he gently shoulder checked Samuel with his own, "Let's get top side."

Samuel shook his head and turned to face Ben, "Just getting a little tight in here, first time jitters maybe."

"You and me both, brother," grunted Ben as he hefted his heavy machine gun and turned to follow the rest of the squad, "I don't know what I expected after signing up, but it certainly wasn't this."

The squad kept moving forward, though their progress was much slower than before, as everyone, including Mag, were on edge and keenly aware that they were not alone. Everyone was exacting in their corner awareness, and Samuel observed from his vantage point at the rear of the group that the effects of their training were beginning to take shape.

During basic, it was very difficult to maintain muzzle discipline, and recruits often would find themselves in the hot box for accidentally pointing their weapons at each other during maneuvers. Here, in the dark mine shafts, with an unknown enemy lurking, the recruits had locked in.

The squad had pushed through another uneventful hundred meters when the hair on the back of Samuel's neck stood up and his heart suddenly began inexplicably pounding in his chest. For the first time in his life, Samuel understood what it was like to be in real danger.

His mouth tasted like he'd gargled with aluminum shavings, and even though the air he was breathing was being cycled through his helmet's respirator, it smelled suddenly sour. He reacted to the sensation by spinning on his heels, dropping to one knee and slamming his rifle to his shoulder.

For a split second his mounted light shone upon the pallid skin of a nightmare.

It was humanoid and stood upright, but he couldn't tell if it had arms, legs or tentacles for appendages. The head was an awful oblong shape that made him want to retch. The eyes burned yellow and by the time it opened its mouth to reveal a sickening maw, Samuel had opened fire.

The marine screamed in a mixture of fear and survivalist rage as he thumbed off his safety and began pounding rounds into the corridor. The creature was blindingly fast, melting into the darkness before Samuel could confirm he'd hit it at all.

"Check your fire and confirm target, marine!" bellowed Mag through the com-bead as the rest of the squad swept their mounted lights across the multiple passages, the standard defensive posture for unknown assailants.

Samuel released the trigger and took a shaky step backwards, only to bump into Ben's shoulder. The gunner was standing perfectly still, facing the corridor down which Samuel had been firing.

Even through the dull red glow of his helmet's internal lighting system Ben's face was noticeably pallid. Both men continued to look down the corridor, but their lights revealed little beyond the crude metal walls and the fresh bullet holes where some of Samuel's rounds impacted.

"Confirm target!" Mag demanded once more from the head of the column, having stopped at a t-section as she briefly looked over her shoulder at the marines filling the corridor behind her.

"Humanoid hostile," uttered Ben in a shaky voice, his machine gun tracking back and forth, as if he expected the creature to leap out of the darkness at any moment, "Humanoid hostile."

Samuel fought to control his breathing. After several deep and steady breaths he was able to stop his body from shaking in the adrenaline aftermath of the encounter.

No longer paralyzed by his own fear, the young man checked his safety and read his ammo count to see that he'd expended eleven high velocity shells. As much as he wanted to swap out for a fresh magazine he could not bear the thought of having an empty weapon even for the few seconds it would take to change the mags.

"I didn't get a good look at it, sir," said Samuel as he found his voice, "Yellow eyes, lots of teeth, possibly multiple appendages."

"Copy that," said Mag as she turned back to the t-section and hefted her combat rifle, "Lock it up, people, this is what we're paid to do. A multi-million credit mining compound doesn't go dark on its own. You see anything that's not a Reaper, you frag it."

When Mag stepped into the open passageway of the t-section a hostile burst from a panel in the ceiling and lashed out at her with an undulating limb as it descended to the floor.

The only person to see it happen in full light was Aaron Baen, who stood behind Mags in the formation. To him, the extremity looked like a barbed whip that bit into the shoulder plating of the boss's armor.

Mag went down as the blow sheared off several pieces of body armor and sent a spray of blood across both Aaron and the wall adjacent. The creature landed, effortlessly absorbing the impact, then sprang forward to pounce upon Aaron even as he brought his combat rifle upwards to meet the threat. The creature's jaws widened and it drove its muzzle toward Aaron's face, smashing through the faceplate of the helmet while the whip-like appendage raked the marine's chest and thigh.

Aaron's vision blurred instantly as his helmet depressurized and the caustic micro-particles that filled the air of M5597 assaulted his eyes. Releasing its jaw's vice-like grip on the helmet it shoved closer in an attempt to clamp down on the meat of Aaron's face.

Before the hostile could find purchase, Aaron squeezed the trigger of his combat rifle and blew out much of the thing's torso at point blank range. When it reared back from the blast, Patrick smashed his boot into the side of the creature's head to force it off of Aaron's ravaged body. The wounded marine dropped his gun and collapsed as Patrick took a step forward to check on Mags.

More screams erupted from multiple passageways, and the marines knew they were surrounded.

"Takeda, hold rear guard position! Patrick on me! Hyst go medic!" shouted Mag as she scampered backwards until her shoulders touched the far wall of the t-section, then she gathered her legs underneath her to rise into a crouched firing position.

No sooner had Patrick leapt over Aaron and joined Mag, than more hostiles began to appear.

The first of them launched itself from the darkness with an inhuman scream as it sprinted down the left corridor of the t-section towards Mag and Patrick, a second one closed in from the opposite direction.

Mag held her rifle steady as best she could despite the deep gash in her shoulder and began firing. The first several rounds went wide until the creature came close enough to strike her again with its barbed appendage. The veteran was able to adjust her aim to compensate for her wound, punching eight rounds neatly into the creature's chest. The first few rounds slowed its momentum and the rest knocked it backwards until it fell to the ground.

Patrick panicked and toggled his rifle to full-auto, pouring firepower down the corridor into the oncoming assailant. His salvo shredded the creature, but as his rifle clicked empty the fallen creature collapsed to reveal a second that had been shadowing it. Patrick took a step back in horror as he fumbled to reload.

"Boss, I'm out!" he shouted as he ejected his spent magazine and rushed to slot another.

Mag groaned with pain as she swept her rifle in a wide arc to point it at the oncoming creature. She kept the gun high so the muzzle didn't cross Patrick, though it cost her dearly in pain, so much so, that her vision blurred. The veteran squeezed the trigger and fired her last three rounds, not knowing if she'd hit the hostile or not as she passed out.

Samuel had rushed to Aaron's side and opened his med-kit. Samuel had earned enough marks during basic to qualify for Reaper duty, though his combat scores were on the bottom tier. With his industrial background it had been decided that he was best suited to being the platoon's medic.

Samuel knelt by Aaron's head and began his process by administering a general booster hypo containing a cocktail of hormones and stimulants that aided in the body's resistance to shock. Salvage marines were exposed to many unknown environments in addition to combat damage, and though each marine represented a minimal investment on the part of Grotto, the cocktail did prevent unnecessary loss of life from shock or infection.

Elite troopers had dropsuits that were, in addition to being high-end body armor, self-contained medical bays.

Each elite dropsuit contained enough food and water for the soldier to survive for several days, on top of containing a full battery of medical hypos, regenerative tissue baths, and, according to the wilder rumors, even stem cells for organ and tissue cloning in the field.

Samuel didn't believe most of the things he heard about how good the elites had it compared to the lowly salvage marines, but after his time in the forges of Baen 6, his experience with medical attention made the salvage marines a definite step up.

Back on Baen 6 a man with the kinds of grievous wounds that Aaron possessed would have been quietly euthanized, either by the foreman or the family, as the kind of medical debts that would be required to save his life would have been beyond the credit lines of most citizens. Samuel could not help but be in awe of the quality of the med-kit he was able to employ upon Aaron's prone body.

Elite troopers were like mythic space warriors, but for Samuel, the Reapers were real, he already had seen more value placed on the lives of these salvage marines than any forge worker.

After the hypo he removed a small sealer pistol, typically used for burn victims, spraying it across Aaron's eyes, hoping that he was able to save them in time for the man to recover his sight. Samuel heard a shout from Patrick and saw the man backing up as he tried to reload his rifle. With Mag passed out, the marine knew he had to get back into the fight.

Samuel dropped his med-kit and launched himself into the t-section, unslinging his rifle. He raised it and began firing on the humanoid hostile. It wasn't until his magazine ran dry that he realized he'd put so many holes in the creature that it was little more than a heap of torn flesh. Patrick stood watch as Samuel reloaded, then the marine returned to Aaron's body.

As Samuel worked on Aaron he could see dozens of spent shell casings and at least one bloody heap lying on the floor of the corridor Ben was guarding. Samuel realized that he must have been so focused on the fight at hand that he'd not even noticed the heavy machine gunner cutting loose with his large weapon.

Using a sealer paste he managed to stop the bleeding and place emergency sutures on the larger gash points in the marine's body, and though he would need major medical attention, at least the man was stabilized.

"Hyst, patch me up and let's get moving," muttered Mag, as she regained consciousness and Patrick helped her to her feet.

Samuel could see that she had lost a tremendous amount of blood. It was a testament to her force of will that she was standing at all. Ben and Patrick did their best to cover all the passageways as Samuel sealed and sutured Mag's shoulder, then he took her combat rifle and reloaded it for her.

"Patrick, take point, you'll need Aaron's rig," Mag ordered as she slung her combat rifle in favor of her officer's pistol. "Samuel, get Aaron on his feet. Takeda, rear guard."

"Sir, all due respect, but I don't think Aaron should be moved," disagreed Samuel as he removed the data rig and handed it to Patrick. "I'd have to pump him full of stims just to get him standing, could have long term adverse effects. I've seen that sort of thing in the forges, when people try pulling triple shifts."

"This is no forge shift, marine. We're at the bottom of a mine in the middle of necrospace," spat Mag as she racked the slide of her pistol to chamber a round and emphasize her point, "We get him moving or we leave him. Profit and loss. Copy?"

"Copy, Sir," said Samuel as he begrudgingly dosed Aaron with three stim hypos and held the wounded man down as his body began to seize briefly while the chemicals did their work. After a few moments Aaron groaned and meekly allowed Samuel to help him to his feet. The burn seals that covered his eyes made him blind, so Samuel had to hold Aaron up and wrap the man's arm around his shoulder. It was awkward, but they managed to fall into formation and begin following Patrick down the dark corridors.

Patrick swept his rifle left and right, up and down, in search of threats. After another fifteen grueling minutes, they reached the main hab doors without further incident.

Ben could have sworn that he'd seen shapes moving in the darkness just at the edge of his mounted light. After the battle in the corridors he was positive that there were, in fact, hostiles pacing them.

As Patrick removed his hand welder, Mag and Ben pulled security after illuminating the area with a flare, slowly sweeping their guns back and forth to cover the three passageways that converged on the gate.

Samuel double-checked the sutures on Aaron's chest and legs, alarmed to see that much of the flesh near the wounds had turned very pallid and a faint green tinge had appeared on the edges. Before he could investigate further, Patrick's welder cut through the lock mechanism.

Samuel gently eased Aaron into a sitting position against the wall, and then helped Patrick push open the hab doors. Ben continued to cover the passages while Mag stood a few steps back from the door as it swung open, prepared to fire upon any hostiles that might lie in wait.

"Hyst, you're with me. Patrick and Takeda hold his position until we give the all clear," Mag ordered as she boldly moved into the hab. "If they want to hit us from the tunnels, now is the best time, so stay sharp."

Mag and Samuel moved into the atrium of the hab and found it to be obscured in just as much darkness as the tunnels had been.

"Talk to me, Hyst, let's see what you can put together," ordered Mag while her mounted light pierced the gloom to reveal that they were in the labor staging area.

Aside from engaging any hostiles encountered during a salvage, it was part of Reaper procedure to investigate the decline of any particular find. In this case, the mining facility had gone dark with little explanation or warning, and though the primary mission was to salvage the station, protocol demanded the establishment of a narrative. Not only did this aid management in their reporting of the haul, but also informed the marines on mission with any additional and perhaps critical details of what they might encounter.

Samuel had trained for this element of the job and had outscored many of the other recruits. It seemed that his time in the quality control division of the forges had given him an eye for minutiae. As Samuel followed his light he took in as much detail as he could see, and began to piece together a possible scenario.

The room had a small catwalk above them that provided access to the various panels and ducts above, presumably for repairs to the hab itself. All around the walls were empty racks where there usually would have been a plethora of mining tools, environmental suits, helmets, and safety cables. There were a few pieces of discarded equipment strewn about the floor, but the majority of the hardware that would be present in a functioning mining compound was nowhere to be seen.

"This is strange. I understand the tunnels being cut off from central power, but most of these hab units have internal generators and backup generators," Samuel observed as he and Mag moved deeper into the building, "Circumstance can knock out the internals, like an earthquake or explosion, whatever, but those backup generators are on a self-contained grid, the only way to shut them down would be manually."

"What about all the missing hardware?" queried Mag as she pushed deeper into the room, "I'm looking for the exit. Do a sight sweep of those catwalks, I don't want one of those things coming down on my head."

"The hardware being gone could mean that the bulk of the workforce were in the tunnels and on shift during the event," said Samuel as he tracked his light over the catwalks, noticing a panel that had been ripped open to reveal the ductwork above. "So, if it was a gas pocket explosion that would explain at least the missing hardware and the internal power being down, mordite gas is rather volatile."

"Wouldn't we have noticed more damage to the tunnels themselves when we infiltrated? Besides, someone locked the tunnels from the inside, we had to cut our way through in the first place," stated Mag as she gingerly checked the handle of the exit door. She nodded back to Samuel and he watched her slowly pull down the lever to open the door, "We also had to cut through the hab door."

"It was like someone started blocking the path into the compound, closing things off behind them," responded Samuel as he began to see where Mag was going with her line of thinking. "So you think they were trying to keep the hostiles out?"

"Or in," said Mag swinging the door open and stepping aside to give Samuel a clear line of fire through the open door.

Gunfire erupted behind them as Ben's voice crackled over the com-bead, "Multiple hostiles closing in on our position, all passageways are compromised!"

"Hyst, hold your position and cover this door, anything moves in there and you blast it!" shouted Mag. She turned to rush back through the atrium toward the tunnel entrance.

"Takeda, lay down suppressing fire against all avenues of approach! Patrick, get Aaron into the hab!"

By the time Mag reached the door, Patrick was assisting Aaron to the ground just on the other side of the door. The chattering sound of Ben's machine gun reverberated through the walls and would certainly have been deafening had it not been for the audio dampeners inside the marine's helmets. Reapers needed full access to their senses, though the helmets were designed to adjust to the environment around them. In many ways, the helmet was the most sophisticated part of the REAPER kit, especially considering that most of the rest of their gear was generic, outdated, or refurbished surplus hardware from frontline military units.

"I'm about to need a drum change, Boss!" shouted Ben as he poured hails of bullets down each of the three corridors. His attacks were answered by the screams of enough inhuman voices that their number was impossible to determine.

Mag knew that once Takeda needed a drum change he would be out of the fight for at least several seconds. Vital seconds since she could see the tangle of limbs rushing at them from the darkness.

"Patrick, get ready to seal the door! There's scrap metal on the floor, cannibalize whatever hardware you see laying around," she said as she stepped up to support Takeda and add her firepower to his.

Mag saw that several drill bits were embedded in the wall and Takeda was bleeding from a ragged hole in his side. The enemy apparently had projectile weapons somewhere out there in the darkness, and as if to verify her suspicion, several more drill bits shot out of the central passageway. Two of them missed and bit into the wall behind her, but one managed to tear through her already wounded arm and gouge a small furrow of flesh from her forearm.

"*Fall back! Fall back!*" shouted Mag as she heard Takeda's gun click dry. She toggled her rifle to 3-round bursts and began to fire salvos down each of the passages to cover Takeda's retreat. Once he was through, Mag turned to leave just as a hostile entered the red light from the flare. The skirmish in the tunnels had been too furious and chaotic for her to get a clear view of their enemies.

In the dull light of the flare she was able to see the hostile from head to toe and recognized the tattered and filthy mining suit that clung to the creature's frame. She screamed and emptied her magazine into the thing's body and hurled herself backwards through the door even as the creature fell away in a spray of dark blood.

Mag lost her footing and fell to the ground as Ben and Patrick slammed the door shut. Patrick turned up the flame on his hand welder and began spot welding broken pieces of mining equipment into the seams of the door. Several more drill bits hit the other side of the door with a clatter, then the screams of several of the creatures filled their ears as fists and who knew what else pounded against the door. Ben and Mag held the door closed as their muscles strained against the hostiles on the other side seeking to force it open. Once Patrick had welded everything he had available to the door he joined them in holding it in place.

"It'll take a few minutes for the welds to cool enough to matter," shouted Patrick as he added his strength to theirs. "We've got to hold this door!"

The screaming from the other side of the door suddenly ceased, individual voices began speaking, even whispering, through the door, as if trying to communicate with the marines inside. If they were speaking a language it was not one that any of the marines understood, though the simple humanistic act of communication was enough to set all of them on edge.

"Ignore it people, it might seem like a nightmare right now, but you'll go through this and worse the longer you sail with the Reapers," assured Mag as she held her part of the door, "This universe is full of nightmares, and as hardcore as these guys are, you will fight worse, and you will win. This is the job!"

"This is the job!" shouted Ben and Patrick simultaneously, joining their leader in the REAPER mantra, soon joined by Samuel through his com-bead, *"This is the job!"*

After several more minutes their attackers either left or at least grew silent, and Patrick nodded.

"That should do it, these welds aren't nearly as strong as the lock we cut, but they'll hold, at least for a while. Assuming the main hab isn't crawling with these things, I can seal up that other door Hyst is covering," said Patrick as he lifted the dazed Aaron to his feet.

"Hyst, you hearing this?" said Mag as she nodded at the rest of the squad, "Let's get behind that second door, we'll sweep the hab and hopefully make contact with the other squads."

"Yes, Boss, I'm hearing. Sounds like we're following the same pattern as the folks before us, sealing ourselves in one layer at a time," Samuel replied as he looked into the gloom of the hab in front of him. "Here's hoping whatever we find in here isn't worse than what's out there."

"Hyst and Takeda, you're on point. Patrick help Aaron and stay on me," Mag said as she began moving forward, her bold strides pushing Samuel and Ben into action to sweep in ahead of her, "Let's get this done."

The squad pushed into the main building. The hab blocks of mining compounds such as this one, were little more than giant cubes, consisting of interlocking buildings that served as living quarters. The hab blocks were mass-produced by Grotto, and were one of the company's major exports, as the demand for cheap housing was high, especially in developing quadrants of the galaxy.

Each standard hab block was designed to house roughly one hundred adult humans. In the design schematics, two children equaled one adult, though the growth and space needs of children were deemed inconsequential to the overall design.

Samuel looked around at the cramped spaces and was reminded of his own home back on Baen 6, certain that inconsequential was Grotto's way of saying "unprofitable".

Each hab block was customizable with a variety of laboratories, workshops, storage lockers, and even prison units. Each of the individual units, regardless of purpose, were connected by a series of sliding doors to the adjacent units and gangplanks to those across. The entire block was a multi-dimensional layering of units and doorways, a veritable maze of gangplanks that rose into the darkness. From the briefing schematics the marines knew that this particular hab block was one of the larger models, and likely extended several more levels upwards beyond the edge of their mounted lights.

"Patrick, get us to the central command unit for block security," ordered Mag as she joined Samuel and Patrick while they paused to take in the vastness of the darkened hab. "A compound this large is bound to have had at least one, possibly two security stations. Population oversight is a big deal on these deep space operations, never know when someone is going to lose their mind out here and need to be dealt with swiftly before they can cause any damage or hurt anyone."

Patrick consulted his rig and found the command unit, dropping a digital pin on the map that allowed him to navigate through the maze using a waypoint. As he further checked the schematics he pointed to two areas on the large scale readout and presented his arm to Mag.

"Squad Marsters was set to enter here and Squad Ulanti here," he said as Mag looked at the rig, "All of the mining tunnels are equidistant from the hab, so unless they got turned around and ended up going down a fabricated shaft that wasn't part of the original compound, they should be converging on the hab bloc by now."

"This is a big place, but sound carries in these things. It's only because of the buzz of people and the hum of the power lines that most people don't notice what their neighbor is saying," added Samuel as he continued to move his light back and forth to scan the perimeter, "Back home the first thing that happens during a blackout is listening to everybody's business."

"You don't realize just how loud people are until they shut up," said Ben as he joined the group, "This place is a tomb."

"Copy that, move out," said Mag, giving the signal to move forward.

The squad continued down the main avenue of the hab as their lights illuminated evidence of one or more brutally violent firefights. The spent shell casings were all shotgun cartridges, the standard issue weapons provided to security forces in Grotto space. The guns and corresponding ammunition were cheap to manufacture and the weapon itself, not to mention the wounds it created, were highly effective in the execution of security operations. Samuel silently pointed out several more drill bits and even a saw blade embedded in the walls, some of which were crusty with old blood.

Patrick stepped in a pile of dung that seemed to have bits of bone and teeth in it. The squad as a whole each gave thanks for the power of their re-breathers to filter out what they imagined must have been a horrible stench permeating the hab. Ben wiped his finger across the guard rail of a gangplank once they'd ascended a flight of stairs to reach the second level and his finger came away with a fine layer of dust.

"Not to be overly creepy or anything, considering what we've just been through, but now that I'm looking at it, this whole place is covered in dust," Ben observed as he looked at the rest of the group.

"So?" said Patrick as he ran his own hand over the rail to see for himself.

"The major contributing factor to dust," Mag said, "in a sealed environment, is human skin cells. We shed more than most folks realize. Sure, it's a mining compound, but you wouldn't have this much of a layer after ten years of being sealed up." She hefted her rifle into a more aggressive posture.

"I've seen this sort of thing on derelict ship salvages. Pretty standard story actually. Malfunction or damage sets the vessel adrift, the air filtration systems stop working even though life support stays active, since it's on emergency backup grids. If there's even one survivor who stays alive on the ship for more than a few months without dying of starvation, thirst, or whatever, then the ship is covered in a layer of dust."

"That's some knowledge that's going to haunt me for the rest of my life, thanks, Boss," piped up Aaron as he lifted his head weakly. Aaron's face was covered in a fine green sheen, as if he'd dunked his face in pond water and come away with a patina of scum.

"At least you're still alive to be haunted," said Patrick as he did his best to smile reassuringly, then to Mag he said, "We're two flights up, one more flight to go then maybe twenty meters and we'll be there."

Progress was slow going, as each marine checked and re-checked their corners, all of them now keenly aware that the creatures could be anywhere, and that someone, somehow, could possibly still be alive inside the hab.

In answer to their silent questions an ear-splitting shriek erupted in the darkness, but it was impossible to tell from what direction it came. It was answered by the staccato pounding of a combat rifle. Suddenly, more inhuman voices rang out of the dark and the sounds of running feet and scrabbling claws could be heard all around them.

"Get up the stairs! I want that security station! *Go! Go!*" bellowed Mag as the squad hustled to follow her orders.

Samuel sprinted up the stairs as fast as his battle armor would allow him. He did not want to get caught in the middle of a firefight exposed on the stairwell, not that the gangplank was much better. The moment he stepped into the open a spinning blade that looked as if it had once been part of a stone-thresher came hurtling out of the darkness toward him. He threw himself to the floor as the blade ricocheted off of the metal girder, throwing out sparks, and clattered over the side of the gangplank.

Samuel rose into a crouch and fired three shots in the direction from which the blade had come, though if he hit anything he couldn't tell. Ben came pounding up the stairs behind him. As he passed Samuel, the gunner thumbed off the safety switch of his weapon.

Running footsteps scraped against the metal of the gangplank as one of the creatures rushed the marines. Combined shots from both Samuel and Ben pitched its body over the rail.

The bestial screams and gunfire continued elsewhere in the compound and soon Mag, Patrick, and a barely conscious Aaron joined the others on the gangplank. They ran as fast as they could across it, with Samuel in the front sweeping his gun in all directions as he looked for possible threats.

As more projectiles, drill bits, nails, and other random bits of twisted metal pelted the area around the squad, frequently pinging off of the marine's battle armor, Mag dropped to a knee and reached for her flares. The veteran started igniting them and throwing them in every direction. Some sailed through the air before falling down to land one or two flights below them while others bounced off of units and landed on gangplanks on their level. One even landed on a gangplank above them. As the boss was throwing flares, the rest of the squad was able to see in the resulting red glow, that the hab bloc was swarming with the creatures.

It would only be in the debriefing, many hours later, that some of the marines of Tango Platoon would recall seeing the creatures actually fighting and killing each other, though in the heat of the moment, all any of the marines could see were swarms of hostiles bearing down on them from all directions.

Samuel raised his rifle and fired several rounds through the back and neck of a creature that was crawling towards them while upside down on the bottom of the gangplank above them. Ben swept his heavy machine gun in a wide one hundred and eighty degree arc as he squeezed the trigger and spit hundreds of rounds at the enemy.

Mag pushed Samuel ahead of her, gesturing to what he could see was the security unit as the rest of the squad rushed for the promise of safety while Ben covered their movements with a withering hail of fire. As Samuel ran, his path was blocked for a tense moment by one of the creatures as it dropped down and landed in front of him. Not breaking stride, he put round after round into the creature. By the time he stepped over its body, the hostile was riddled with holes.

Now that they could see the enemy more clearly, Samuel was convinced that these creatures had once been the mining crew. Nearly all of the creatures wore remnants of either environmental suits or Grotto civilian clothing.

Patrick shouted and pointed, revealing Squad Marsters as it fought its way up the stairs from the East. As he did, one of the hostile hurled a spinning blade that slammed into his back. Patrick's battle armor protected him from being wounded by the blade, but the impact knocked him to the ground. Aaron was too weak to stand and had been using Patrick as support. Robbed of that, the wounded marine collapsed in a heap on top of his comrade.

Aaron rolled onto his back. Even though he was completely blind he clicked off the safety of his combat rifle and started firing single shots down the gangplank in the general direction of the enemy. The hostile wasn't hit by Aaron's rounds, but the marine's sporadic fire distracted it long enough for Mag to put a well-placed round through its skull.

Samuel turned and rushed back to help Patrick to his feet. The two men dragged Aaron behind them as Ben covered the rear and Mag took point. The veteran tried the door and found it locked. Instead of trying in vain to shoot through the security glass, she turned to Patrick.

"We'll hold here until you cut through the door. Might take a moment, but once we're inside we can set up a real fighting position." She raised her rifle to fire on a hostile that looked like it was taking aim with some kind of modified power tool. "Standard issue habs all have the manual emergency generator stored inside the security unit, so if somebody turned it off on purpose we can turn it back on. I'm tired of fighting these guys in the dark!"

Samuel noticed that the flares Mag had thrown were beginning to dim, so he took a moment to hurl two of his own before shouldering his rifle and continuing to fire once more. Ben's heavy gun clicked dry and he dropped it to the floor, drawing his sidearm even as the red-hot barrels of his gun sizzled against the blood and dust that covered the gangplank.

Squad Marsters finally emerged from the far stairwell and began fighting their way towards Squad Taggart. Harold Marr's machine gun must also have been out of ammunition, since he had slung it in favor of his sidearm. Other than that, the squad was at full fighting capacity and seemed to have sustained zero casualties.

With the added fire support, the marines were able to drive back the onslaught of the creatures. Patrick gave a shout and backed away from the door as the now molten metal of what had once been the lock slid to the floor. Mag nodded at Samuel and the young man rushed forward to stomp kick the door open as he held his rifle pointed upwards.

Jada Sek, the new recruit from Squad Marsters, rushed into the unit with her combat rifle in a tight grip. As soon as she passed him, Samuel lowered his rifle and rushed inside after her, allowing the two marines to breach the room while having almost all of the angles of fire covered. The maneuver saved their lives, as they were immediately rushed by a hostile that had apparently been waiting inside the unit.

The hostile's appendage lashed out and jerked the combat rifle from Samuel's grip even as it body slammed Jada into the far wall. The creature rammed its muzzle into Jada's chest and began tearing through her armor with its teeth.

Without thinking, Samuel slid his salvage tool from its strap, roaring as he shoved it into the hostile's body. His momentum was totally concentrated at the tip of his salvage tool and he hit the creature hard enough that despite the blunt edge, he was able to savagely impale it. Samuel held his grip on the tool and stepped to the side, pulling as hard as he could, wrenching the hostile away from Jada and sending it crashing to the floor. Jada stepped forward and screamed as she fired several rounds into the beast.

Samuel and Jada both stood over the body of the creature, breathing hard, captivated by the stained, but unmistakable, Grotto environmental suit that clung to the creature's warped body. It wasn't until Mag shouted over the gunfire that the two marines snapped out of it and returned to the fight.

"Hey Prybar! Quit standing around with your mouth open and get the damn power turned back on!" yelled Boss Taggart as she stormed into the small compartment while slotting in a fresh magazine. "We're running out of ammo out here, so we gotta make our shots count for a hell of a lot more than they are now! Move it, soldier!"

Samuel yanked his salvage tool from the creature's body and crept further into the security compartment. Jada had loaded her last magazine and covered his advance from a few paces behind him. They were met with no additional hostiles and after a painstaking search through the darkness, illuminated only by the half-light of a flare that Jada had thrown ahead of them, Samuel finally found the manual generator.

In the tiny room someone had written the words, "In Everyone", using what appeared to be a mixture of blood and feces. Samuel was able to find the primary breaker and worked quickly to activate the generator. His father had shown him a trick or two as a young boy, and thanks to cheap Grotto inventory controls, the old generators that were used in the forges were rotated out into the deep space mining compounds.

No doubt the various engines and generators used by the fabricators and engineers in Assemblage 23, where Samuel's father had worked until his death the year before, were much newer than this. His father had worked on such machines in his youth, and for all Samuel knew, this very piece could have come from Baen 6.

After several tense minutes of tinkering, Samuel managed to reconnect all of the appropriate valves and cables that had been haphazardly disconnected by whomever had shut down the power all those years ago. The generator coughed several times, stiff from disuse, finally growling to life. The grid indicators began to switch from red to green. The complex began to light up one level at a time, beginning with the first.

Samuel and Jada rushed back to the front of the security compartment to find that the entire complex was now lit up. Track lights and work lamps bathed the entire compound in a dull yellow glow. From his vantage point Samuel could see dozens of the creatures, some on the walkways, others clinging to the walls and ceiling, many of them carrying old mining equipment that had been retro-fitted to function as projectile weapons.

At first the sight of so many of the enemy was intimidating until Squad Marsters and Squad Taggart opened up with renewed vigor at an enemy they could finally see clear as day. Samuel recovered his combat rifle and stepped out onto the walkway to add his fire to the rest of the marines.

As he tracked and eliminated his targets Samuel could see that Squad Ulanti was moving down from the top of the complex, driving the enemy towards them. What had begun as a desperate running battle for survival became a slaughter as the marines mercilessly shot down the creatures.

After a re-supply mission delivered fresh ammunition and with the addition of Magna Platoon as reinforcements, the Reapers were able to rapidly clear and secure the compound.

Bravo Platoon joined them shortly afterwards. While Tango Platoon nursed its wounds, the new platoons spent an entire second standard day cycle sweeping the mining tunnels and eliminating the remaining hostiles. Despite being outnumbered and outgunned, they continued to fight back with a primal tenacity and cunning that cost several more marine lives.

The after-action report and final debriefing postulated that the M5597 compound encountered a rare bacterial infection, amplified by the unknown affects of an environment filled with both mordite gas and biridium that directly affected the DNA of the mining staff.

Samuel had thought it was an awfully callous way of describing the transformation of the Grotto employees into rampaging monsters. Judging from the evidence they found in the compound and the tunnels, the welded locks, the lack of power and the various signs of armed struggle, the transformation had not affected everyone at the same time. It was clear that the staff had mutated at different rates, with the entire complex becoming a battleground between the transformed hostiles and the staff, only for the staff to eventually transform and turn on one another after they'd sealed themselves in.

It was unclear how many survivors had escaped the compound aboard the starship. No staff were present in the crew manifests of the Red Listed ship that had been recovered. Their fate would remain unknown.

It appeared Grotto was going to chalk up the complex as a loss and have the entire facility scrapped instead of attempting to re-open mining operations. Samuel left the debriefing having been told that the Reaper fleet would remain in orbit for an estimated two months as the marines switched over from combat duties to salvage operations.

Samuel was perfectly fine with that, having no desire at that moment, to ever take up a firearm again.

It wasn't until he was back in the compound, after the rush of battle had faded, that Samuel realized he'd left Aaron unattended and leaning up against a wall.

Apparently, at some point during the violent chaos, Aaron had bled out through a deep puncture in his side. Samuel could not recall if he'd had the wound before or after the marine had set him against the wall and that not knowing troubled him deeply. Casualties were to be expected, according to the debriefing administrator, and this was the first hot mission for the Baen 6 Reaper fleet.

Regardless, Samuel could not shake the sick feeling in his stomach.

REST AND REFIT

The marines were housed near the aft of the ship in a series of suites, commonly referred to as "racks" by the people who lived in them. Each suite consisted of two rooms, each room housing a pair of roommates and each block of ten suites shared a single shower and bathroom facility.

Samuel was still feeling shaky and nauseous from the ascent shipside, and though he'd already been to the mission debriefing and had plenty of time to re-adjust to the artificial gravity of the ship, he couldn't quite feel at ease.

Twice in one mission he had come close to dying and although he had faced a number of industrial accidents without injury, the prospect of immediate death by violence was new to him. He wasn't sure how he expected to feel after his first hot mission, but the tightness in his chest and the knots in his belly seemed at once too much and too little. It was as if a pressure was building up inside him that demanded release. Samuel entered his room just as Oliver was leaving, and the marine grabbed Samuel by the shoulder.

"Oh no, you don't, marine! Nobody just showers and goes to bed their first night shipside after a mission," Oliver informed him jovially, as he spun Samuel around and pulled the young man along with him back down the hallway, "Especially after your first mission! Time to get a load on!"

"I'm not much of a drinker, Oli," argued Samuel meekly as he let himself be dragged alongside Oliver. The two men turned the corner and walked down the gangplank towards the mess hall, which doubled as a cantina during the evening cycle. "I'm still kind of twitchy from the fight, you know?"

"Look kid, a few cocktails and you'll even out, that's kind of the point," chuckled Oliver as they entered the cantina.

The room was packed tighter than Samuel had ever seen it during mess hall hours, but he immediately saw his squad mates as they offered up hearty cheer. What they said he couldn't make out through the din of the other sixty odd voices. Ben saw them coming and waved Samuel and Oliver over to the handful of tables they'd pushed together.

All of the surviving members of Tango Platoon were present, other than Mag, who was no doubt still in the med-bay. Before Samuel could say a word, Jada shoved a shot glass in his hand and playfully pushed his hand to his mouth so he would be forced to swallow it.

The drink was semi-sweet, as if it was distilled from a fruit of some kind, but it burned like fire on the way down his throat.

"To the face!" shouted Jada as she picked up a bottle and poured another round, which she then handed to Samuel and Oliver, keeping one for herself. "We were waiting to toast the fallen until you guys got here."

Wynn Marsters and Lucinda Ulanti, were sitting next to Jada. Wynn nodded at Lucinda and the veteran stood up as she addressed the cantina.

"Salvage Marines! Form up!" she bellowed across the room, instantly silencing the other voices.

Samuel watched the bosses of the other platoons and their squad leaders leap to their feet, quickly followed by the rest of the recruits in the room.

"I speak for Tango Platoon," Boss Ulanti said, raising her glass. "Tonight we drink to the early retirement of Yvonne White and Aaron Baen. They stood by our sides and paid the price so we didn't have to." Boss Ulanti swept her gaze across the room and back down to her platoon, "This is the job."

With that Lucinda and the rest of the marines in Tango Platoon knocked back their shots and again Samuel's throat burned, though this time not quite so fiercely as it had before. He was still blinking back tears from the stoutness of the alcohol when another boss stood up, one who he did not recognize.

"I speak for Bravo Platoon. Tonight we drink to the early retirement of Max Baen, James Horlick, and Mitchell Sanders. They stood by our sides and paid the price so we didn't have to." The unknown boss held up his glass, "This is the job."

It continued like that until all of the platoons had named their dead, and by the time it was over the shots were going to Samuel's head and he was thankful for the opportunity to sit down.

The rest of the evening seemed to go by increasingly fast, and as he drank and joked with his platoon mates he found that the tightness in his chest had abated. The knot in his stomach seemed to lessen with each drink he knocked back. Soon he was caught up in the fervor of celebration alongside his fellow marines, and he found he recalled less and less of the horrors of the mission they had completed.

At some point in the night he realized that Jada was kissing him. Though he'd been intensely attracted to her since basic training, not once had he imagined actually touching her. Samuel thought of himself as an honorable man and he'd made a vow to Sura when they'd been married.

However, with his passion inflamed by combat and the fact that he had survived, not to mention heavy drink, the planet of Baen 6 seemed terribly far away. There was a beautiful woman kissing him and she was right there, she was real. Eventually Jada led Samuel by the hand to her suite, and in the darkness of her bunk they made desperate and life-affirming love.

As the morning cycle transitioned into the day cycle Samuel shuffled into the mess hall still shaking the cobwebs from his brain and feeling as if his mouth had been stuffed with cotton. He had awoken in Jada's bed extremely hung over. His companion from the night before was polite enough, she had made it clear she intended to sleep off her equally powerful hangover and had little interest in conversation.

Samuel entered the food line and the server piled his plate high with powdered eggs, fried protein paste, and several of the strange citrus fruits that smelled as if they'd been the same fruit the booze was distilled from.

He took a seat in an empty corner of the mess hall. At that hour it was not overly crowded. Most of the ship's crew were already on shift and the majority of the marines were likely still sleeping off the prior evening's revelry.

Typically, marines were not allowed such luxuries as sleeping in since training regiments were part of daily life, even when in transition between missions. Samuel dimly recalled being told the night before, that the first night shipside after a mission, the combat troops were given a day's rest to recover, both from their mission and resulting celebrations.

Samuel did his best to fight the nausea as he tucked into his meal, though the more bites he took the better he began to feel. He was in the process of quaffing his third mug of water and his second plate of food when Mag sat down at his table. She too had a plate piled high with processed food, though Samuel could not help but to notice that her left arm was no longer entirely normal.

Mag looked at him and followed his gaze, then grunted and revealed her hand. The entire arm had been amputated at the shoulder and replaced with a crude robotic arm. The quality of the prosthetic limb was appalling, considering the technology of the age, and Samuel's mouth was agape.

"Yeah, it's a hunk of junk, isn't it?" said Mag, understanding Samuel's look of shock. "The doctors gave me the choice between a model covered by the universal marine triage plan or one of the high end models that I'd have to borrow on my credit line for."

"No offense, Boss, but I've seen better arms on labor droids," admitted Samuel as he did his best to return to his meal and not stare at the claw-like fingers that clumsily grasped Mag's water mug. "Is our health plan that bad?"

"Well, this is Grotto kid," grumbled Mag as she shoveled down a mouthful of eggs, "They don't get all that imaginative with naming things, so if a plan has the word 'triage' in front of it, you can assume it isn't going to be designed with your best interest in mind." She shrugged. "This happens all the time. A marine gets some serious combat damage and the choice is a crappy triage treatment or a chance to have the cutting edge stuff. If I'd been willing to take on a ton more debt, I could have an arm that looked identical to my old one, tattoos and all. Or I could have opted for a servo arm that I could mount tools on. The possibilities are as big as your credit line, and a veteran who has been around as long as I have has a big damn credit line."

Samuel frowned. "I get not wanting more debt, but-" he began before Mag cut him off.

"But, nothing. I've paid off the life-bonds of my son and both my grand kids. Paying off mine is just a few pay cycles away," Mag explained, pausing to take a bit of fried protein paste. "So, as long as I can avoid any more of Grotto's sneaky little debt traps, I'll be able to retire in a year or two with enough credits to die in relative comfort."

"I wish I had things figured out like that. It seems like the longer I do this the more confusing things get, and I've only been doing this for a few months," Samuel muttered as he toyed with the last scraps of his meal. "Everything is upside down."

"Keeping things confusing is good for the bottom line, that's part of Grotto's game, hell, that's part of it for every corporation, company, and cartel from here to the other side of the universe." Mag set her fork down and looked directly at Samuel. "Just do your job, don't sustain any major wounds, and don't forget for a second that you are completely on your own. To the company you're just a resource, no different from bullets, trucks, or raw minerals. Keep your head on straight and maybe you'll walk away from the game with more than you came with."

Mag got up from the table and put her tray in the receptacle before turning to Samuel.

"Don't beat yourself up about Jada," said Mag as she awkwardly clutched his shoulder with her clawed robotic arm, "Everybody knows about it, you two weren't all that smooth about making your exit."

"I feel like an idiot and a philanderer," admitted Samuel, rubbing his temples with his fingers, as if trying to clear the memory of her, however sweet it might have been.

"You are a philanderer, that's true, but you're also a soldier, and soldiers fight and die a long way from home. When you're that close to death, sometimes you need to get it on with someone who knows what you're going through, just to prove you're still alive. I'm not saying it's right or wrong, I'm just saying that it happens, and just like a stout drink, it keeps you steady." Mag began walking out of the mess hall. "I'm sure Jada needed it as much as you did, hell, most of you new recruits probably bunked up last night. It's just how things are."

Samuel finished his meal and returned to his suite, his mind swimming with memories of the evening's recklessness. His roommate, Oliver, was still snoring when Samuel climbed back into his own bunk. With his pen light and a data pad he began to write a letter to his wife, to tell her of his first mission and to express his doubts about joining the marines. However, after nearly an hour of struggling with what to say, he deleted the letter and shut down the data pad. Mag seemed to be correct. Even in his attempts to write down what happened, he found the boundaries of language too limiting to communicate clearly what he was feeling or what he had seen.

Silence, it seemed for now, was the only honest choice.

SPACE HULK

"As you can see from the surveillance photos, the squatters have grafted much of the hulk together, using spot welds and even high tension cables to further bind the various pieces of the ship," said the shift manager as she used her remote to zoom in on one particular portion of the massive ship. "Intel advises that this particular vessel is our most effective means of entry."

Samuel looked at the vessel, a yellowed, oblong ship of a sleek design that he'd never seen before. Though Samuel was in no way a master of ship identifications outside of the Grotto hive fleet with which they had been serving for the better part of the last year, he did recognize the Praxis Mundi logo etched into the side of the ship.

Praxis Mundi was a long range shipping company that made regular runs into the Baen system. The company was a smaller player in the galactic trade wars and tended to operate as a neutral shipping option for companies and individuals moving modest volumes of cargo extra long distances.

Next to Samuel sat Ben, who was engrossed in the briefing and taking notes as it went along. Ben had never paid this much attention in academy and it was evidence of a much larger change in the man. They were only a year in and it had already been a hard tour. Change had become part of the daily struggle.

After the mission on M5597, the Baen Reaper fleet had been assigned to leave the 5500 sector and rendezvous with Grotto Hive Fleet 822 for an extended mission. The hive fleets were essentially mobile factories and refineries that move from region to region within Grotto space.

The fleets would strip entire worlds of their natural resources, then after a few months or years, they would move on, leaving the planet to its fate. The fleet carried only a modest military element since it was not a frontline endeavor, however, it did travel with a small contingent of security forces that operated out of a single, mid-sized battle frigate.

In the event of a full-scale engagement, the fleet would undoubtedly succumb to a professional combat force, though the single frigate was sufficient to ward off any pirates or Red List ships that might prowl the space lanes.

Samuel was later informed that some one hundred or more standard years ago, Grotto had engaged in a major trade war with Aegis Inc. over a somewhat remote solar system that was, at the time, thought to be rich with natural resources.

After two years of bitter conflict Grotto withdrew from battle. The board of directors determined the war had reached a point of diminishing returns against the projected profits to be yielded from the resource exploitation.

For Aegis Inc. it had been a pyrrhic victory. They had committed so much money, manpower, and material to the war effort that despite their 'victory' the mining and harvesting operations continued to operate in the red. After another five years of dwindling profits and relentless raids by Red Listed pirates, the entire sector was abandoned and had sat idle for a full seventy years.

Aegis had maintained a loose picket of the sector with a few frigates, though even those were finally pulled back.

Grotto, while not interested in permanent occupation, had seen an opportunity to exploit the now lawless and undefended sector. Hive Fleet 822 was dispatched to plunder the system, and at the vanguard of the fleet's advance would be the Baen Reaper fleet.

With the entire sector having been classified as necrospace, the corporate protocol demanded that Reaper elements sweep, clear, and salvage it as part of an overall reconnaissance mission to support the hive fleet.

Those orders had come down nine months ago and since then Samuel and the salvage marines had been marching through the dead system. For the most part the missions planetside had been general sweep and clear engagements met with little resistance beyond the occasional squatter community.

Most of the time the various facilities and factory outposts were completely abandoned. The salvage marines were free to chop the scrap and haul it to the tug ship without firing a single shot. Samuel, like the rest of the recruits, had become quite expert at operating forklifts, gravity cranes, and hand welders.

Tuck, a marine from Squad Ulanti, had taken to calling the hand welder the true symbol of the salvage marine, not the death's head image that was etched into their ships, weapons, and armor.

There had been a handful of violent encounters over the past months, though none as savage as the campaign on M5597. Red List ships made regular runs through the sector. It was a convenient shortcut between various corporate held territories for those ships and individuals who sought to remain outside said corporate notice or attention. Due to the traffic flow, a number of squatter communities had sprung up as the otherwise nomadic space folk who lived on the fringes of human society claimed the abandoned buildings as their own.

While most ships and communities scattered and fled at the approach of the Reaper fleet, some of the squatters rejected the notion of "corporate salvage rights". Those few squatters who chose to fight were quickly routed by the salvage marines, and generally after the initial firefight, most would lay down arms. One void battle with the Reaper frigates that destroyed several Red List ships was all it took to send a clear message to everyone in the sector to vacate or be destroyed.

It had sickened Samuel to drive people out of their homes, more so when he had to shoot squatters, which he had done on three separate occasions. Though as time passed, Samuel found that the continued soldier wages and hazard duty bonuses stacked up higher than his compassion for strangers, so, for the sake of his family, he hardened his heart. As Ben had begun to say, there were only two kinds of people in the universe, those behind the gun and those in front of it.

Samuel's thoughts were grim as he recalled Ben's words. Watching his friend take notes, he found that he begrudgingly agreed. He wondered if Sura could see the world in such stark contrast, and smiled to himself as he acknowledged that, of course, she couldn't. Her unassailable optimism was like a beam of light that seemed to be able to touch him in his darkest moments while in the depths of necrospace. For her, and for his son, he could be a soldier and a provider, even if that meant other people, like the squatters, had to be pushed out of his way.

With the hazard pay and soldier wages he'd earned in the last year he had paid off half of Orion's life-bond. He would have already paid it completely if he had not been required to make minimum payments on his own life-bond. Now that Sura was nursing a newborn at home they'd decided that she should leave the workforce, so Samuel was covering her minimum payment as well. It tore him up to have only seen his wife once in the last year since joining the marines. His son was in his third month of life and Samuel had never physically seen him, but it felt good every time a pay cycle would hit.

A new photo was illuminated on the shift manager's display and Samuel looked away from Ben's notes to see a wide-angle shot of the full space hulk. He'd always heard of their legendary size, had even seen photos, but seeing one that he knew he was about to assault was awe inspiring.

Hulks were colossal conglomerates of miscellaneous space junk that had, over countless years, become so large they acquired their own gravitational pull that drew in even more flotsam. Hulks usually began their lifecycle as single ship, typically large freighters or tugs that, for one reason or another, ended up dead and floating through space.

Other ships, satellites, and various bits of scrap would collide with them and either become embedded in the larger ship or hovered nearby in a tight orbit. Over years and years more bits would collect until the gravitational pull would hold the whole thing together.

Space Hulks were both a sought after prize and a likely deathtrap. Because they were comprised of so many ships, in addition to assorted space junk, they were often rich with salvage. Because of the haphazard method of their creation, the hulks could be affected by any number of dangers. Many were filled with toxic chemicals, fuel spills, breached and radioactive engine cores, and destabilized heavy machinery.

In addition to those risks, there was always the likelihood that portions of the hulks were populated by various organisms.

Squatters from the Red List would often seek shelter in the hulks even though scavengers and pirates frequently made raids into them for resources, scrap, or to carry off the squatters. There were also rumors, blasted as tall tales, about insectoid alien creatures that infested some hulks, using them like massive nests. (Though there was no official Grotto statement as to the truth of any such claims.)

As Samuel looked at the photo he could see several gun emplacements bristling along the more stable sections of the hulk and he leaned over to Ben.

"From the looks of those guns I'd say we're going up against a pirate clan, not squatters," he whispered.

Ben nodded, "Calling them squatters must be more politically correct. I don't know why they bother, we're going to fight them, one way or the other."

"Personally, I'd rather them just say pirates, at least then we'd be more prepared," grumbled Samuel, despite the fact that he was having difficulty in not being both excited and terrified at the prospect of carrying out a boarding action.

"Hulks & Pirates," whistled Harold Marr quietly, a marine from Squad Marsters, who sat behind the two friends, "Man, I used to play that game with my brothers. I think I might even have a few of the action figures in my closet back home. This is surreal."

"Me too, I always pretended to be the Pirate King," Jada agreed from where she sat next to Harold, directly behind Samuel, "None of the boys could handle the crown."

"So does that make Tuck the Queen?," said Ben amiably as he leaned back in his chair to smile at Jada.

Samuel and the rest of the small group shared a quiet laugh as Jada blushed and gently kicked Ben's seat before she joined in the laughter.

It had taken Samuel several months and a few more firefights to clear his conscience of his tryst with Jada.

After their very next mission, the first of the Hive Fleet 822 operations, he had taken a bullet in the side before gunning down two squatter resistance fighters as the marines were sweeping a small communications facility.

Squad Ulanti had been down in the power plant and encountered similar fighting. Both he and Jada had sought the now familiar comfort in each other's naked embrace after the fight. After that time, however, both of them had discovered a growing awkwardness, as if being together once more had changed their lovemaking from celebrating survival to something more towards romance.

Samuel had felt ashamed of himself, and it seemed that Jada has as well, for she and everyone else in Tango Platoon knew Samuel was married and had a newborn. After that uncomfortable morning another two months of operations passed before the two of them spoke to each other again. Though now, over nine months into the campaign, they had found space for friendship.

Samuel slotted his magazine and racked the slide on the combat rifle, chambering the first round as he let his breath out slowly. Tango Platoon was only moments away from boarding their assault craft and despite his months of combat duty this would be his first boarding action. It was the same for the majority of the rest of the salvage marines in the Reaper fleet, since only their squad leaders were veterans.

There were a handful of exceptions, like Oliver Putin, who were survivors of other Reaper fleets that had been liquidated. Samuel looked out across the hangar bay of the great Reaper tug ship and saw that dozens of platoons also stood in tight rows as they, too, waited to board their respective assault craft.

Finally, warning klaxons began to sound while yellow and red lights flooded the hangar bay. Mag walked down the line of Squad Taggart, double checking their void gear and giving them last minute pointers on the coming fight.

"Void battles are fought in a full three hundred and sixty degrees," barked Mag, raising her voice to carry over the engines of the assault crafts as they revved to life. "No doubt the hulk has artificial gravity in some sections, but you need to be prepared to fight in zero gravity. You've all had void combat training during basic, but for most of you that's nearly a year in the past. If Grotto cared more about making an investment in our continued survival they would have issued this boat with a training deck, but seeing as how they didn't, we aren't and this briefing is as good as you're going to get."

Samuel listen with rapt attention. He'd heard many tales and stories about void battles. Tales of the unfathomable emptiness of space, the fragility of the very ships upon which they rode, and the surreal silence that accompanied even the most brilliant of conflicts.

The marine could feel the additional weight of the void seals that had been screwed into the sockets of his standard issue battle armor. All marine armor came pre-drilled and threaded to support additional void equipment which made Samuel think that it would have indeed been wise to provide them more training for void combat during basic. He'd learned the hard way though, over the last many months of his tour through necrospace, that Grotto Corporation only cared about human life in so much as it affected the Bottom Line.

He understood that it was a grim view of the world, and one that he'd neither explained to Sura, nor even attempted to make her aware of. In many ways, he felt that being in the Reaper fleet had opened his eyes profoundly to the vast and uncaring world of Grotto Corporation more than any of his time in the factories.

It was as if by being a Reaper he was able to look down on the rest of the world from a high enough vantage point to see the totality of the organism otherwise known as Grotto. A multi-galactic corporation that spanned through countless systems, ruled over the lives of billions, but most importantly, was only one of a multitude of such companies. Perhaps Grotto was the largest, but it was certainly not the only predator stalking the fields of the endless trade wars.

The Reaper fleets were accorded equipment that was either well-used, refurbished, decommissioned, or cheaply acquired from Grotto subsidiaries. The marines themselves were recruited from the lowest class citizens in the corporate civilization and offered pay far beyond what they could hope for in the civilian workforce. Their primary mission was to roam the galaxy and pick up the scraps left in the wake of corporate progress.

This is the job, he told himself as he returned his attention to Mag, who was discussing the vagaries of zero gravity firefights.

"Though your weapons all have recoil dampeners, firing them in zero gravity is going to push you around just as hard as if you'd kicked off a wall," said Mag, "So be sparing with your shots and stay aware of who is around you." The ground guide crewman gave the all clear signal with his lightstick, "Okay, then, salvage marines, let's saddle up and get this done!"

Samuel loaded in next to last, with Ben bringing up the rear. The heavy machine gunner was unable to bring his standard issue weapon on a mission such as this due to the possibility of causing critical internal damage to the hulk during combat. Though the entire hulk would eventually be scrapped, it would be counterproductive for an errant armor piercing round to strike a fuel line or gas pocket deep within the hulk. Secondary explosions, as they were informed by Mag, were the second leading cause of death for boarding parties entering combat on unknown vessels. The first leading cause of death was being gunned down during the blistering first few seconds of combat when the assault team made shipside.

As a counter measure, Ben, in addition to the other heavy gunners in the salvage marine boarding force, had been required to trade out his machine gun for a breaching shield and assault shotgun. The shield, when held at a ninety-degree angle out from the chest, would cover Ben from mid-shin to the top of his head. The shield was strong enough to repel most small arms fire, so as long as the enemy wasn't packing anything bigger than a combat rifle Ben had a reasonable expectation of pushing through any possible hail of fire. There was a small bulletproof viewing slot at eye level, which, while not nearly as strong as the metal of the shield, could certainly still deflect all but the most accurate and direct impacts. Just above chest level was a gun port through which Ben would be able to point his shotgun, which would rest on a small gun mount in the port that allowed him to re-cock the shotgun simply by pushing forward and letting the shield rack the slide.

Standard tactical boarding procedure was for the shield bearer to exit the assault craft as soon as the blast doors opened, then as the marine pushed forward, he or she would rapid fire the twenty-round shotgun magazine. Once the shield bearer had drawn enemy fire and begun to engage, the rest of the squad would fall in to support until resistance was quelled and a beachhead established.

"You ready for this, brother?" asked Ben as he sat down next to Samuel and began to strap in while he rested the giant shield against the nearby wall.

"I should be asking you, Ben, this is going to be intense," Samuel responded as he double-checked his straps, and then gripped the handle of the boarding knife affixed to his forearm. "Since when do they issue us extra close quarters weapons?"

"Yeah, boys, this is gonna get nasty," added Oliver, who sat opposite of Samuel, "These boarding knives aren't part of standard issue kit because typically we don't end up getting close enough to use bladed weapons. Well, except for maybe Prybar over here."

The seven or so members of Tango Platoon who heard Oliver's joke laughed, even if their voices were tinged with nervousness. Mag sat in grim silence, but nodded just the same. The nickname 'Prybar' had stuck with Samuel ever since the sweep and clear on M5597. Samuel laughed with his comrades, as he figured that it was pretty good as far as nicknames went, and after all, he had earned it.

"Lots of times these kind of ship-to-ship assaults can throw some close quarters fights at you. A ship doesn't seem all that complicated until you're engaging hostiles, maybe in zero gravity, on an unfamiliar boat with lots of hidden corners, narrow hallways, and who knows what else in there," said Oliver as he slid the nine inch blade from the sheath on his forearm. "Some space pirates don't even bother with guns on board ship, just body armor and these beauties."

"Putin, that's enough," ordered Marsters as he went down the line of his squad checking their harnesses and helping Harold slot his breaching shield into its fixed position on the flat edge of the man's seat, "You're scaring the rest of the children. Everybody just keep your eyes open, stay tight on Takeda and Marr. We'll get through this."

Wynn Marsters walked back to his own seat and strapped in as Squad Ulanti filed in and took their seats near the back of the assault craft. The plan was for Tango Platoon to use the heavily armored prow of the assault craft to punch through the hull of the Praxis Mundi ship, somewhere near the foredecks. Squad Taggart and Squad Marsters would be in first to fight for the breach and establish a beachhead, then Squad Ulanti would pick up their momentum and make the first real penetration into the hulk. Squad Taggart and Squad Marsters would take a few precious moments to assess casualties, triage wounded, and re-arm before falling in behind Squad Ulanti. They would move as a platoon to sweep and clear the Praxis Mundi vessel of hostiles. Once control of the ship was taken they would establish and secure any entrances to the greater body of the hulk.

Dozens of other platoons would be engaging in similar boarding actions throughout the space hulk, some focusing on taking the larger and more intact vessels that comprised the hulk while others would target and eliminate the various artillery and heavy guns that would be defending the hulk.

Samuel was sure, as were many of the other marines, that several of the ships that appeared grafted onto the space hulk were actually temporarily docked. If this was indeed a functional pirate hulk, as the marines suspected, and not a scrap ship that had been picked up by the hulk's gravitational pull, then they were looking at encountering heavy resistance. Only time would tell, and according to the mission clock displayed above the airlock the time was swift approaching.

Samuel's stomach lurched as the assault craft kicked on its engines and plunged into the void. The marine closed his eyes and thought about the hazard pay and the life that he'd dreamed it would buy for him and his family. He knew it was still just a dream, acknowledging that it was simple escapism. He knew that within less than three minutes, according to the mission clock, he would be leaping into battle with pirates in the depths of necrospace.

As if to calm his mind, as well as the others, the voice of Mag rang out on his com-bead, "This is the job."

"*This is the job,*" responded the voices of fifteen salvage marines as they hurtled through the void towards the hostile scrap metal monstrosity.

Within seconds of hitting void, their assault craft was under fire. While the hulk was bristling with heavy guns that were easily visible, dozens of smaller weapon systems abruptly came to life across the expanse of the hulk. The pirates had been prepared for a troop assault, be it from corporate military forces or simply rival pirate clans.

From concealed positions flak-launchers and plasma-lances opened up on the flights of assault craft. The void of space between the Reaper tug and the hulk was soon bursting with thousands of tracer rounds, flak detonations, and spears of concentrated plasma as the hulk showed its teeth and defended itself. The Reaper tug carried only minimal defensive weapons, none of which would have any effect, especially at long range, against the heavy gun emplacements of the hulk. It was up to the two escort frigates to dart in and attack the guns before speeding back out again. Their armor and energy shields were insufficient to protect them from any direct hits so speed was paramount.

The naval crews that operated the combat frigates of the Reaper fleet were predominantly veterans from other military forces within the Grotto organization. Soldiers who had chosen Reaper duty over retirement or mustering out with disabilities, so the tactics employed by the light combat ships were effective and expertly executed.

While the assault craft were too small and moving too quickly to be effectively tracked and fired upon by the larger guns, the plasma-lances became particularly deadly as the craft closed distance with their landing targets.

The cloud of flak detonations damaged and disabled a number of the assault craft, leaving them floating in space and unable to maneuver, making them easy pickings for the plasma-lances. Several of the assault craft suffered direct hits from pinpointed plasma bursts. The impact crumpled the hull armor and allowed the super-heated plasma to turn everything inside the ships to ash before explosive decompression blew it apart.

When the assault flight finally passed through the flak cloud it had suffered nearly a fifteen percent casualty rate. Now though, the ships that made it through the picket line began to slam their prows into the hull of the massive conglomerate to disgorge their troops into the belly of the beast.

STORM AND VOID

Had Samuel been able to witness the void battle taking place it would have been one of the most beautiful and terrible sights of his life. As it was, he knew nothing of the dramatic events playing out around him. His awareness was limited to the grim faces of the fourteen other salvage marines of Tango Platoon as their ship rocketed towards the space hulk.

The lack of sound in the vacuum of space gave no indication of the carnage unfolding around them beyond the occasional ding of flak particles stinging the hull of their assault craft. The mission clock had been reset on launch to show distance to target, so that each marine could mentally prepare themselves for what was about to come.

Samuel tapped his boot on the floor and watched the distance rapidly approach zero, then, as it hit zero the entire ship shook and lurched. The prow of the ship had broken through the hull of the Praxis Mundi vessel and lodged the ship firmly in the skin of the vessel.

Theoretically, there would be a temporary vacuum seal thanks to the bulk of the assault craft jamming itself into the metal of the enemy vessel, though, because of the inevitable rate of decompression, at some point the seal would break.

The strategy for all boarding actions was to have the assault vehicle penetrate the ship deeply enough that the boarding party could seal one or more airlocks behind them as they fought their way into the ship. This would allow two of the three-person crew of the assault craft itself to don void suits and use their welding gear to cut the assault ship free so that it could return to the tug. If the boarding party was victorious, the assault craft would hold its position until relief troops could be ferried over. If the boarding party was defeated, the assault craft would be free so that it could escape, with or without any of the boarding party survivors, depending on the conditions of the engagement and the temperament of the craft's pilot.

Mere seconds after the craft slammed into the space hulk, pressurized blast doors slid open and the automated seating units began disgorging the marines into the landing zone.

Each seat at the front of the column, starting with Ben and Harold, swiveled to face the exit and sprang forward to launch the marine off the ship before folding in on itself to make room for the next seated marine. In this way the ship was able to rapidly deploy two full squads in a matter of seconds.

Samuel's breath was labored and he worked to calm himself down as the squads rushed across the shattered landing zone. Before the marine could even begin to gain an appreciation for the area in which they'd landed, the squads were under fire.

Ben's shield rattled from the impact of hard rounds as they blasted into him from a number of directions. Ben shouted as he fired the breaching shotgun as fast as he could, joined by Harold who was also emptying his firearm with abandon. Samuel saw several hostiles scampering through the stacks of metal containers while they took potshots at the oncoming marines. He raised his rifle to return fire. By the time one went down in a spray of blood, he had already turned his rifle to the next target before the corpse of the first had hit the deck.

Ben and Harold led the charge from behind their shields as they fired and Samuel stayed close behind his friend, moving from side to side and firing from Ben's flanks as the team pushed through. The combined forty rounds of buckshot from the shield-bearers, with support from the rest of the squad when and where they could get a clean shot, cleared the immediate vicinity as the marines rushed forward to take and hold a series of stacked metal containers.

Samuel, through force of habit long ingrained in him, checked his safety and ammo count. He was surprised to see that without realizing it he'd expended nearly all of his magazine, and it was only then, in the brief calm amid the violent storm, that he was able to take stock of his surroundings.

They were in a large compartment of the ship that appeared to be storing a vast hoard of shipping containers. They all had different corporate logos, makes, and models, proof that these pirates had been active and successful for a long time.

As expected for a pirate crew defending their stash, there was stiff resistance waiting for them. The pirates had to have known that this would be a prime target for the assault craft and had bolstered their numbers in the area.

Samuel could see that while plenty of broken corpses littered the deck, there were still several clusters of hostiles wearing their own patchwork battle armor rushing into the fight.

While many of the defenders were in plainclothes or general deckhand garb, those who did wear some type of battle armor all bore the same half-moon symbol painted or etched somewhere on their outfit. Though Samuel did not recognize the symbol, it did tell him that indeed this was an organized group and not at all the 'squatters' described in the briefing.

While Ben and Harold reloaded, Samuel looked around at the rest of the marines, performing a casualty assessment out of habit. While he'd never been awarded a command, he had learned from Mag that constant evaluation was key to a complete victory.

It was then that Samuel noticed Oliver Putin's corpse some ten meters away, only a handful of steps from the now empty troop bay of the assault craft. In the midst of the firefight he must have taken a stray round to the head. Samuel could see the smoking, ragged hole in the man's helmet. Oliver wasn't even the first man out of the craft and he'd still been killed. The randomness of it bore down on Samuel's mind like the crush of a black hole. It was only the ringing boom of a round striking the metal container he was crouched behind that pulled him back into the moment.

These were hardened space pirates with plenty of experience in repelling boarding actions and their strategists seemed to have predicted this area as one of the targets for the salvage marines. Several shooters had taken up high vantages on the tops of containers several meters away and began pouring suppressing fire down on Squad Taggart.

Ben kept Samuel and Patrick alive with his shield as the marines scampered for cover. A group of defenders rushed the marines in an attempt to flank and route them and it looked for a moment as if the momentum of the boarding party was about to be stopped cold. The defenders fired as they ran, apparently not as concerned with accuracy as much as they were with keeping the marines pinned down while they pushed forward. Somewhere out of the chaos Mag appeared on Samuel's right side, hurling a frag grenade over the top of the container towards the approaching forces.

Samuel was shocked to see that Mag had broken combat protocols by even having the grenade in her kit, much less deploying it before the squad was able to secure a beachhead with an air seal.

"Boss! That explosion could depressurize the whole compartment!" shouted Samuel, forgetting her rank in the heat of the moment.

"Ben, you move when I move, and don't stop for anything!" barked Mag, ignoring Samuel and gripping Ben's shoulder with her robotic arm, "Now!" Mag pushed Ben ahead of her, out of their dubious cover and he did as he was ordered.

Samuel, still bewildered, but determined to follow orders, fell in behind Mag as Patrick and the new guy brought up the rear.

Samuel had never bothered to learn the new guy's name, especially since he was the second man to replace Aaron Baen on Squad Taggart. The first new guy had been named Michael, though his last name was lost to dim memory. Michael had taken a high velocity crossbow bolt through the neck several months ago.

It had not been a particularly dangerous operation, just a sweep and clear of a small drilling platform. The squad had encountered a clan of squatters who had taken over the drill, managed to get it running again, and were extracting ferrite ore, which they no doubt sold on the black market. The marines came in with enough of a show of force that the squatters gave up without a fight, instead choosing to flee.

Sadly, there had been one squatter, a rather old man, who refused to back down. Before the marines shot him to pieces he managed to send Michael into early retirement. Since then, Samuel just hadn't taken the time to learn the new guy's name, as if anyone who wasn't with him in Basic just didn't merit a name. Oliver had told him this often happened with soldiers, no name, and no attachments. Staring at the body of the veteran lying cold on the ground, Samuel understood.

Mag's grenade had sailed out from her position and landed among the defenders as they sprinted toward the marine's. When the grenade landed among them, the tight formation scattered, abruptly ending their suppressing fire. This gap in the shooting allowed Ben to emerged from behind the container and give the rest of the squad time to form up behind him. Ben rushed forward as he rapid-fired his breaching shotgun to shred several of the pirates as they reacted to the simultaneous threats.

Mag and Samuel fired from Ben's flanks and were able to drop more of the defenders while Patrick and the new guy fired as needed to keep random lone attackers from sweeping in behind the squad.

The marines sliced into the defender's position and scattered the enemy. Ben knelt down behind his shield, working swiftly to reload his shotgun with the final magazine as the squad took up fighting positions around him. Mag's charge had placed them right in the middle of the compartment, and they immediately began to draw sporadic fire from a multitude of directions. Despite their gains the boarding party's momentum was again threatening to slow, as the squad swiftly became mired in a shootout from all sides.

Samuel realized the grenade Mag had thrown hadn't gone off, suddenly appreciating the brazen brilliance of the tactic. The grenade hadn't been primed and was never going to explode, though in the rush of the conflict the pirates had assumed it would blow. Anyone would, and that was the trick.

Across the compartment, the bodies of pirates littered the ground, swimming in a sea of blood, scrap metal, and shell casings. Despite all the gains made by the marines, the pirates were still managing to hold the compartment with bitter resilience. Bullets rang off the metal containers as both forces fought their hardest.

Samuel felt hard rounds bite into his armor and turned to see that a pirate wielding a combat rifle had opened fire on their position from atop a container. The new guy's body was riddled with bullets as he and Samuel returned fire, killing the pirate.

Samuel looked down at the young man's broken corpse and felt a sudden guilt in not learning his name. Suddenly, Samuel heard, then saw, Squad Marsters, which had disappeared on the left flank seemingly ages ago, join the fight and make a bold move.

"Fight through!" bellowed Boss Marsters as his squad appeared on the left side of the compartment. While Squad Taggart had held the attention of the bulk of the defenders, Boss Marsters had quietly and quickly moved his troops down the far wall, no doubt fighting their way there, though not through the kind of firefight Mag had taken her people through.

Squad Marsters, led by Harold and his punishing rate of fire, slammed into a small cluster of defenders who had erected a makeshift barricade next to the main airlock. The furious barrage of buckshot kept the pirates at bay until Harold reached the barricade.

As Virginia shot down a pirate who tried to fire down on them from the top of a container, Boss Marsters leapt over the low, makeshift wall and knocked several hostiles to the ground as he fell. Behind him, Jada vaulted in and buried her boarding knife in the neck of a pirate who was attempting to raise his pistol to shoot the Boss. The young marine drove the point of her knife through the back of another pirate who was attempting to rise, then Boss Marsters was on his feet and swinging his own blade.

One of the pirates was wearing body armor and wielding his own wide-bladed knife, which he used to parry the Boss's blade before catching Jada's on his armored forearm. The pirate blocked another strike from Jada and managed to push her blade aside before stepping inside her guard and ramming his knife through her chest. The titanium blade punched through her battle armor and as the pirate pulled his blade out there was a brilliant spray of blood.

Harold screamed as he finally reached the fighting and smashed his shield into the pirate, knocking the man over. Harold pinned him down with the shield and Boss Marsters was able to end the pirate's struggle by sliding his blade under the armpit articulation in the man's armor and into his heart.

Samuel's heart skipped a beat when he saw Jada go down and he found himself blinking back tears of rage as he sighted down his rifle and sent three rounds into the chest of a fleeing pirate. Mag shouted for the squad to advance and they pushed forward to join Squad Marsters at the airlock.

If they could take and hold the airlock, then Squad Ulanti would be on the way to support them and make the first real incursion into the depths of the space hulk. The few defenders still alive had dug in the far right corner of the compartment.

Virginia and Mag crept through the mess of containers in the shattered hangar bay to engage the last ditch defenders while the rest of the marines worked on breaching the airlock.

Patrick used his hand welder to burn through the bottom while Boss Wynn used his to come in through the top. Between the two of them they'd cut through the mag-locks in just over a minute.

Samuel knelt at Jada's side and worked frantically to save her life. She was gasping as she looked pleadingly at Samuel. To the marine it looked as if the young woman had been stabbed through the lung and might have a chance of surviving if he acted quickly enough.

He opened his med-kit and found the emergency lung. He gritted his teeth as he slid the nozzle and feeder tube into her ragged wound without giving her painkillers, which might have hampered her ability to breathe by relaxing her. In this situation he needed her to be as agitated and awake as possible, despite how much it might hurt.

Once the nozzle was inside her punctured lung, Samuel hit the inflator and the emergency lung, contained in a small plastic box that he attached to her armor with the adhesion strips on the bottom of the box, the artificial lung began to inflate her real lung. Once that was done Samuel used the hypo multi-tool to inject a vial of faux flesh into the wound. The faux flesh would seal the wound and keep her real lung from re-collapsing.

His work was good, and soon Jada was stabilized enough to let her be. She would need to go to med-bay as soon as possible, and could still die from shock and complications if the boarding party did not conclude their business soon. For now, Samuel had done what he could as a medic, and he unslung his rifle in preparation to do what he could as a soldier, which was to secure the beachhead and take the space hulk.

Mag and Virginia took turns firing and moving as they advanced on the five remaining pirates who defended the landing zone. Once they were within shouting distance Mag gave them a choice.

"Listen up, space scum!" shouted Mag as she slotted another magazine and chambered the first round, "We are taking this ship one way or the other. The only choice you have now is whether you die in this room today or take your chances in the penal labor system. What's it gonna be?"

"Sod off, company man! We're nobody's slaves!" shouted one of the pirates from behind cover.

"Have it your way," grumbled Mag. She grabbed a frag grenade and yanked the pin, letting it cook for a few seconds before throwing it, all while a visibly shocked Virginia watched.

"You're crazy Boss, you know that right?" said Virginia, crouched with Mag behind cover while the pirates shouted in surprise at the grenade landing in their midst.

"Now that we have a beachhead the hard part is done, I'd rather blow another hole in the ship than get killed at the last minute trying to take out stragglers," Mag snarled before smiling wickedly as the frag grenade detonated, giving the pirates a grisly end.

Harold and Ben, each on their last shotgun magazine, stood ready to enter the airlock as Boss Marsters and Patrick pulled it open. Samuel had gently moved Jada to the side, just under cover of the makeshift barricade. Once the doors opened the two shield bearers leapt through the threshold and into a brutal firefight. Pirates had positioned themselves on either side of the corridor and were using scrap metal pieces in the hallways to create modest cover for themselves.

However, in the tight metal passageways, the breaching shotguns of the salvage marines revealed their truly devastating capabilities. As their shields bucked against the impact of enemy fire, the marines rapid-fired their shotguns with Ben taking the right passage and Harold taking the left. In the tight environment, the buckshot rattled and ricocheted to create a deadly cloud of projectiles that shredded defenders on either side of the corridor.

Those who weren't killed outright were either wounded or driven back. Samuel fell in directly behind Ben, who, once his shotgun was empty, knelt to allow Samuel to stand over him. The shields all had a gun rest built into the top so that marines could execute this very maneuver.

Samuel was protected from the upper chest down while he rested his weapon on top of the shield to keep it steady as he fired upon the enemy. Boss Marsters performed the same maneuver with Harold on the other side. The marines paused to allow Mag and Virginia to join them, and each of the three person teams moved forward to the next hallway. At that point they slotted fresh magazines and held their position. The marines had expended all or most of their ammunition by that point, and though the fighting had only been going on for a few minutes, each one of the marines was exhausted by the furious pace of the battle.

"Squad Ulanti, beachhead is secure and you are clear to advance," reported Mag as she scanned the hallway in front of her.

Samuel knew that just beyond their sight would be more pirates working to rally their defenses and prepare for the next phase of the battle. However, now that the beachhead had been established it would be tremendously difficult for the pirates to push the marines off the ship.

As Squad Ulanti pounded across the compartment floor to reach the airlock, Samuel wondered how the dozens of other boarding parties had fared in their initial assault. How many marines, he wondered, were now crawling through the insides of the space hulk?

When Squad Ulanti arrived, they carried with them several boxes of additional ammunition. For ten anxious minutes the new squad held the line while the survivors of the first two squads reloaded their magazines.

Once everyone had re-armed, Squad Ulanti pushed forward as what was left of Squad Taggart held the right corridor and Squad Marsters held the left. Lucinda led her squad down the main corridor and was immediately met with stiff resistance.

Samuel could hear shouting and shooting from his position behind Ben's shield and found himself counting the seconds until they could advance. He felt, deep in his bones, that to stop was to die, and according to everything he'd been hearing about boarding actions, this was accurate. Boarding actions were inherently an all-or-nothing scenario, with the percentages of survival dwindling the longer the defenders were able to hold out.

There would be no re-supply mission, so the marines had to take the ship with the ammunition that they'd brought with them. The crate hauled in by Squad Ulanti held two full reloads for each member of the squad. The ammunition would go slightly further than it might have otherwise, as both of the assault squads had suffered casualties. Samuel looked back over his shoulder to Jada's prone form, watching while she struggled to breathe. Even with the apparatus she was still in danger.

After what seemed like hours, but was only a matter of minutes, the shooting abated.

"Boss Taggart, the way ahead is secure, you can move up," crackled Boss Ulanti's voice over the com-bead, her transmission somewhat distorted by the hulk. Because the gigantic craft was a conglomerate of untold numbers of other ships and various pieces of space flotsam it was anyone's guess as to what might be causing the interference.

Mag nodded at Samuel, who turned and tapped Ben on the shoulder, then the three marines moved through the corridor to join Squad Ulanti. Behind them, Squad Marsters spread out their defenses to cover both corridors. From here on out Harold, Virginia, and Boss Marsters would hold the beachhead. Assuming the other marines were successful and the ship was taken, then Wynn would move his people deeper inside to help secure the area and begin the salvage. Until then, Squad Marsters would serve as a rearguard, plugging the gap they'd smashed in the enemy's defenses so that the marines pushing forward couldn't be attacked from behind. Samuel appreciated the tactic, although knew from the additional briefings from Mag that more often than not, once the boarding party was far enough from the beachhead anything could happen.

The ship was a maze of corridors, compartments, and hostiles, and nothing could be trusted except the marine to the fore and the marine to the aft.

Samuel gingerly stepped over the bodies of several pirates as he, Mag, and Ben joined the other marines.

"They've pulled back for now, not sure if they're routed or if they have something else planned," said Boss Ulanti as the marines reached her position.

"They pulled back fast once we hit them, and I gotta say Boss, none of the compartments we've passed have that "squatter digs" look to them," observed George Tuck, the rig operator for Squad Ulanti. "I'm thinking this ship is functional. Might still be grafted to the hulk, but my guess is, this one isn't derelict."

"I know you guys thrashed the place, but the landing zone looked to me like a functioning warehouse. I used to run a lifter on Baen 6, I'd know," pointed out Andrea Baen, another orphan who had been recruited from Baen 6 at last year's founding.

"Keen point, marine," said Mag as her eyes scanned the ship's interior before them. "If the Praxis Mundi specs are accurate, and the pirates haven't made too many modifications, we should only be one compartment block away from the prime deck. We clear that and we'll control the core of this vessel."

"That'll be a bitch to hold with so few of us," said Spender from the front of the group as he held his combat rifle pointed down the corridor.

"Taggart is right," agreed Boss Ulanti. "We take the center and bring Squad Marsters up, then any other marines who've been able to push inside should end up converging on us." She hefted her combat rifle and began to march forward. "Check your corners, conserve ammo, and let's get this done. Move out."

Samuel and Ben looked at Mag and she nodded. Ben moved to the front of the group so that he could cover their advance alongside the marine who had replaced Yvonne White on Squad Ulanti.

Samuel again realized how few names of any of the replacements or new recruits he knew, as if only the fifteen marines who were with him in Basic could occupy space in his brain. It was a mental oddity, though from what Mag said, it was very common among marines who had been on the job long enough to lose comrades. It seemed like such a callous thing that his mind would perform such unconscious mental triage.

The journey through the next compartment block went without incident. Samuel agreed with Tuck that the ship was in fairly good condition, all things considered. Most of the holds were full of crates, shelving units, and barrels that supported the idea that while this was no longer a ship capable of deep space travel, it had certainly been kept functioning.

Samuel imagined that life on board a space hulk might hold all manner of surprises for those desperate or courageous enough to attempt it. When he recalled the sheer scale of the hulk he realized that once the marines had taken this Praxis Mundi vessel there would still be plenty more work to be done. The Reapers could seize a ship a day and the fleet would still be moored in the hulk's presence for easily a month or more as they plumbed the depths of the great beast. All in all, Samuel was beginning to understand the cruel brilliance behind the Reaper fleet's deployment upon such missions. The amount of potential revenue that could be generated from the ship salvage and space scrap alone was enough to pay for the fleet's continued presence. Any losses incurred while taking the hulk, including expended ammunition, damage to assault craft and marines killed-in-action, would be more than recovered by any additional materials discovered on board the hulk.

"I get why management has us hitting this ship first. It isn't about a strategically positioned beachhead," Samuel said to Mag as they crept forward through the storage compartments towards the central deck. "It's because long range sensors could tell that this ship still had artificial gravity, power sources, and before becoming part of the hulk this ship was a transport hauler. It's safe to assume that with the pirate presence here they'd be storing plenty of food, equipment, loot, or whatever on board."

Mag snorted with quiet contempt. "You're finally catching on kid. This hulk is so big there isn't really a strategically sound insertion point. You just pick a spot and dig in. It might as well be where the best salvage is sitting."

The marines reached the entrance to the central deck and immediately Ben and the other shield-bearer began taking fire. The marines pushed through the corridor into the open deck and found themselves on the high deck with another deck below them. Samuel was reminded of the retail complexes back on Baen 6 where everything was designed to allow the pedestrian to view the storefronts on both decks from a high vantage point.

The marines kept close to the shield bearers as they hugged the wall on the right so that they could stay out of the field of fire from the gunmen below while engaging those on the high deck.

As the marines fought their way forward across the high deck the sounds of more shooting elsewhere in the central area erupted. Samuel recognized the unique sound of the standard issue Reaper combat rifle, then the telltale report of the breaching shotgun and knew that other marines had stormed the area. Samuel surged with confidence and aggression as he realized that his small band of marines were no longer the only ones in the fight, and that other boarding parties had managed to work their way to the central deck. He was not alone in this feeling, and the change in posture and disposition amongst the other marines was palpable.

"Weapons free!" shouted Boss Ulanti as the marines spread out across the high deck and began engaging targets as each marine took up individual fighting positions.

Samuel braced his rifle on the railing of the high deck and aimed down at the pirate gunmen below. The marine drilled several bloody holes in the back of a pirate sniper who was firing on the advancing marines from the other platoon. After he shot down a second pirate, Samuel saw an access hatch blow out and through the smoke strode another squad of Reapers, who immediately added their firepower to that of their comrades.

The shooting intensified as more marines and pirates emerged from various corridors, side hatches, and gangplanks. It seemed that both the marines and the pirates agreed that controlling the central deck was the key to controlling the ship.

Andrea joined Samuel on the rail and the two of them worked the actions of their rifles, steadily pouring rounds at a cluster of pirates who were attempting to mass for a counter-assault on the newest squad of marines to leap into the fight.

Suddenly, a tremendous explosion rocked the entire ship, and the shockwave of the blast knocked most of the combatants to the ground.

"What the hell was that?" shouted Spencer, sprinting to catch up with Boss Ulanti, who had also been knocked onto her back by the shockwave, "Feels like the whole ship is keening!"

"That's because it is!" boomed Boss Ulanti's voice over the com-bead, "Activate your void armor *now!*"

Samuel had landed on his chest and was shocked when pushing himself up actually sent him flying up away from the floor. Andrea was shouting below him as he soared away and it took his back slamming into the ceiling of the central deck before Samuel realized the artificial gravity was gone. He depressed the activator button on his neck to ignite the void seals. The armor would protect him from the hard vacuum of space for a short time, but he realized with stark terror, that the void armor was absolutely useless in helping him navigate in zero gravity.

Samuel's disoriented gaze swept across the central deck to see the ship slowly spinning in a wide circle around the hapless floating marines and pirates and he realized that gravity was the least of his worries. The ship had clearly broken free of its moorings to the space hulk by whatever the explosions were and was now tumbling through open space.

"We still have a job to do people! The tug will recover us if we can clear the ship! So fight, damn you! Fight!" roared Mag in everyone's com-bead as the veteran pushed off from the wall and went sailing across the central deck. Her trajectory took her over the position of several pirates who were struggling to regain their footing. The veteran fired several rounds into the pirates as she sailed over them and turned her body mid-flight so that when she hit the opposite wall she was able to break her impact with her boots.

Samuel pushed off the ceiling and took aim as best he could at a pirate floating nearby. The recoil dampeners in his rifle prevented the shooting from altering his course more than a few feet. He was able to land on the high deck's floor even as the pirate's bullet riddled body spun away in a tight circle that sent globules of blood flying in all directions. Andrea was using one hand to grip the rail and hold herself in place while she took carefully placed shots at various targets with the other hand.

Samuel moved to join her, but was knocked off of his feet by a hard round that impacted his chest plate. Thankfully, the bullet did not penetrate his battle armor, but it hit hard enough for Samuel to saw stars for a few seconds and left him unable to prevent himself from crashing into the wall behind him.

Andrea grunted in pain briefly and Samuel saw long streaks of blood jetting out of her as a pirate who floated above her fired dozens of rounds from a short-barreled submachine gun.

Samuel snapped his combat rifle to his shoulder and emptied his last four rounds into the pirate. The marine reloaded and gently pushed off from the wall to reach Andrea's corpse. Samuel was down to his last magazine and he knew that the dead marine had at least had one fresh one. He felt odd about how quickly he'd overcome witnessing her death, though he knew that to hesitate in this sort of environment was suicidal.

The marine sighted down his rifle and looked out over the battlefield to witness a roiling three hundred and sixty degree firefight as the pirates and marines careened across the deck. He saw Boss Ulanti, who had apparently abandoned her combat rifle, sail across the central deck and swipe the head off of a pirate using her boarding knife. The man's head and body went spinning away in opposite directions passing another pirate and marine locked in mortal combat with their own blades. It was madness, and the marine knew that standing still would make him an easy target. Samuel took a deep breath, unsheathed his boarding knife, and then pushed off to send himself careening into the melee as he fired.

Nearly twenty hours later Samuel, Ben, and Virginia walked from their barracks to the med-bay looking for Jada. They were politely informed when they inquired at the exterior waiting room that the marine was making an effective recovery, but was being sedated for the next several days as the various machines worked hard to repair her damaged lung. Boss Marsters emerged from the interior waiting room and nodded at the three marines as the doctor retreated back into the med-bay.

"Jada Sek is one tough soldier, she's going to pull through," Wynn Marsters assured the marines. "Like the doc said, they're having to keep her sedated, the machines are doing what they can for the lung, but over the next few hours they are going to remove the damaged one and insert a nu-flesh lung."

"Excuse me, sir, isn't nu-flesh hugely expensive?", asked Virginia as she and the other marines exchanged confused glances. "I thought only elites and management could afford that kind of medical treatment."

"Yeah, I figured they'd just stick an auto-inflator in there and be done with it," said Ben, "Our standard Reaper policies don't cover nu-flesh."

"They don't, Takeda, and yes, Tillman, the nu-flesh organs are top of the line bio-ware, and Jada is going to have a mountain of debt to pay off for medical treatments outside of her standard plan," agreed Boss Marsters as he sat down in one of the uncomfortable waiting room chairs and began to rub his temples, revealing the fatigue of the last several days, "And before you ask, yes, I was the one who authorized the procedure. Pursuant to REAPER Battlefield Protocol 16, the commanding officer assumes decision making responsibilities for a marine's medical care if that marine is in critical condition and unable to communicate with the attending medical staff."

"So you just decided that she was going to incur another debt that she's got to pay back?" asked Samuel, with more heat in his voice than was wise considering who he was speaking with. Wynn Marsters' face darkened instantly with anger.

"Hyst, and the rest of you, had better listen up," said Boss Marsters in a low growl, "Until your time with the Reapers ends, your lives are in the hands of your squad leaders, and believe it or not we want you to survive.' He paused and drew a breath before speaking again.

"Let's say I decided to save Jada some money and she got the auto-inflator. We all know those things are fragile and prone to breakdown, so she'd have to get it replaced every year or so, and the standard plan doesn't cover replacements. That means that she would either incur more debt buying the replacements or she would just go on living with one lung. I need a marine who isn't going to get winded and out of breath in the middle of an engagement. I need a marine who isn't going to take a few slugs to the chest and pass out because the armor impacts disrupted the inflator. And believe me, Jada doesn't want that either, even if it means she'll have to put in more time on the job to pay it down."

Boss Marsters stood up and stormed away, but just before he reached the exit the squad leader turned around. His expression softened and he said, "We are soldiers, and that means that people get killed and people get hurt. Everyone knows that the standard Reaper plan is garbage and everything else is astronomically expensive. There is no middle ground. That's life in the Grotto Corporation, and this is the gamble we make to earn the Reaper pay rate. None of us would be here if we were satisfied with our workforce assignments, so remember that we all chose to be here and to assume the risk."

After Boss Marsters left the room the three marines were grimly silent, each lost in their own thoughts, until George Tuck emerged from the interior waiting room.

"Hey guys, glad you came to check in. I figure you heard what Marsters did?" asked George as he joined the small group.

"Just told us, crazy stuff man, but he's got a point," said Virginia as she put an arm around George to comfort him. "She's going to pull through just fine, and so what if there will be a ton more credits hanging over her head. We could all die tomorrow."

"You have a weird way of trying to comfort people," laughed Ben as he started walking towards the door. "Tuck, we're gonna hit the cantina, you should come."

"Seriously, George, this is going to be our one night of leisure before that space hulk consumes our very existence," grumbled Virginia amiably as George nodded his head and let the marines lead him away from med-bay.

Samuel hung back, staying a few paces behind the rest of the marines, lost in thought. Mag had warned him about the medical risks one took when getting wounded on the battlefield, though he couldn't fault Boss Marsters for wanting the best for his wounded marine.

Jada had not been the only casualty of Tango Platoon in the last twenty-four hours. The new guy to Squad Taggart, whom Samuel had found out from Mag was named Kristoph, had bought it along with Oliver during the fight for the landing zone. He'd watched Andrea Baen gunned down right before his eyes, while both Lucinda Ulanti and Spencer Green had been sent to med-bay with various cuts, bruises, and bullet holes. He tried to solace himself with the knowledge that it would take some time, but Jada, Spencer, and Boss Ulanti would all be back on duty soon enough, he thought to himself as he followed his friends.

He understood the desire to have a few strong drinks, especially after the harrowing twenty-four hours he had just experienced. It wasn't until the debriefing that it had really sunk into his mind just how incredibly lucky he, or any of them for that matter, had been to survive.

While the salvage marines had been fighting their way through the Praxis Mundi ship, one of the concealed pirate cruisers had fired up its engines and launched a counter-attack on the Reaper tug. The pirate vessel was not sufficiently armed to do any crippling damage to the heavily armored tug ship, though it certainly could have prevented the second wave of assault craft that were ramping up to launch. Without the second wave for support, the first boarding force of marines would most certainly have run out of ammunition, suffered horrible casualties, and likely have been swallowed by the hulk.

If the hulk was not taken in a boarding action, the Reaper fleet would have had to pull back and wait for a Grotto warship to arrive with artillery capable of simply blasting the hulk to pieces. Doing so might preserve the lives of hundreds of marines, but a boarding action was the only way to secure the hulk for proper salvage.

During the artillery exchange between the pirate cruiser and the Reaper security frigate that moved to intercept it, there was an explosion. At the time of the debriefing it was not known whether the explosion was caused by ordinance from the nearby void battle between the cruiser and the frigate. It might have been charges placed by the pirates to intentionally render the Praxis Mundi unsalvageable, or perhaps simply a mechanical accident. Regardless of the cause, the ship was ripped from its moorings by the explosion and had tumbled through space, losing its artificial gravity, followed only minutes later by power, and thus life support.

The furious zero gravity combat had raged on for several more minutes. When the lights went out the fight was done in sickeningly close quarters. Samuel, even many hours later, still found his hands shaking at the thought of what it had been like fighting the last pirate, out of ammunition and his combat rifle forgotten somewhere in the darkness of the ship. Spears of light shining through the viewports of the central deck, in addition to the sporadic flashes and lights from the receding void battle offered the only occasional glimpses of the battle.

Samuel still had his light in one hand and his boarding knife in the other when a pirate barreled into him from behind. The two men had careened through the deck as each slashed and stabbed at the other with his respective blade. After a few intense moments, Samuel was able to score a deep gouge through the man's inner thigh. The pirate's arterial wound had sprayed blood that that instantly crystallized and it was the sight of scarlet crystals shattering against his helmet's faceplate that had chilled Samuel to the core.

Mag had always warned him that it was the little details that would drive a man crazy if he didn't deal with them. So that night Samuel was determined to tell his friends the story and get it out into the open. By the time he did, everyone was drunk enough to laugh about it. There were more psychologically responsible ways to cope with such things, Samuel had found himself thinking, but this was certainly more fun.

The marines enjoyed their time in the cantina, knowing that at the start of the next day cycle the salvage of the space hulk would begin.

Rough tonnage estimates, not accounting for unknown factors or additional resource discoveries, placed the salvage time at six standard months. The marines would be swapping out their battle armor and combat rifles for hazard suits, welders, and lifters. There would still be security patrols, since the massive structure no doubt still housed pockets of pirates and squatters who were not killed in the fighting, or had chosen not to turn themselves in.

Samuel knew that most of the pirates and squatters would end up being shipped to one of the many penal colonies operated by Grotto. Even the humans who called the space hulk home were considered revenue-generating resources to be salvaged, tallied, and redistributed.

At the end of six months, where the impossibly large space hulk had once drifted through space, there was little more than a small cloud of debris.

TETRA PRIME

Samuel was jostled in his seat as the combat speeder wove its way through the ravine; a jagged furrow torn through the land by eons of flowing currents. The waters of the planet known as Tetra Prime had long since been siphoned away, leaving the former sea beds to bake in the punishing light of the triple suns that illuminated the Tetra star system.

From his seat Samuel could see through a small viewport and his breath caught in his throat as the combat speeder exited the ravine to reveal hundreds of miles of sandy valley floor below. The mission briefing had educated him on the history of the planet and current military objectives, but the sheer power of humanity's ability to change a planet had not been presented to him so dramatically as it was in that moment.

As Samuel looked out at the valley it was hard to believe that only one hundred twenty-seven standard years ago this planet was a single vast ocean, the only surface land being a handful of wave-battered islands.

According to the briefing, Grotto purchased the planet, along with half of the rest of the Tetra system, from Rubicon Enterprises at a bargain price. Rubicon had liquidated the entire system to fund a distant trade war and expansion campaign several galaxies away. Rubicon had been using Tetra Prime as an untapped water reserve, and though they had leased fishing rights to several small operations, the impact on the marine population was minimal considering the size of the planet.

When Grotto Corporation took over the planet, the resource giant had bought out the fishing leases and installed a number of pipeline hubs on the scattered islands. These pipeline hubs drew raw water from the oceans, filtered out the rocks, sediment, and marine life from the water and stored it in massive containers. The containers would be loaded onto cargo haulers that would move back and forth between the hubs and the truly gargantuan deep space transport ships for which Grotto was famous. The transports would then move the water throughout Grotto space to feed the various needs of the company.

With corporations engaging in business across such vast tracts of mapped space there were billions of thirsty citizens, hydro-electric plants, and various other industrial efforts that required staggering amounts of the precious liquid.

Grotto Corporation, which had a well-deserved reputation as a voracious destroyer of worlds, cared little for engaging in sustainable environmental practices. In as few as ninety two years the entire planet's oceans were sucked dry and as much as ninety five percent of the planet's water had been harvested and taken off-world. The rapid change in the planet's mass had altered its gravitational and magnetic properties. What had once been a planet with a relative fifty percent sunlight and fifty percent darkness relationship with its triple sun swiftly tilted on its axis. The new orbital pattern bathed the majority of the planet in the scorching light of at least one of the three suns at all times, leaving a small portion of the planet in perpetual freezing darkness. With the marine life extinct, no standing water beyond a few frozen lakes on the dark side of the planet, and nothing else left to take, Grotto had abandoned the planet.

The speeder came to a stop at the mouth of the ravine to wait for the rest of the column to enter the ravine and muster at the mouth. The engines of the speeders caused too much vibration for more than one to go through the ravine without causing seismic signatures that could be read by the security sensors likely being used by the enemy to defend their newly seized prize.

Samuel looked down at the center of the valley and took in the sight of the colony. The name of the colony was unknown to him beyond the designation RLC5611, which stood for "Red Listed Colony", this one being the five thousand six hundred and eleventh recorded by Grotto. Samuel doubted that many of those recorded colonies still stood since it was the standard policy for Reapers to forcibly remove them from salvage sites.

Though he had participated in driving out a number of squatter communities from valuable salvage sites during his time with Hive Fleet 822, many more were recorded that later disappeared into the void or were taken by pirates.

Red List ships and settlements were notoriously difficult to keep track of, especially since few in the corporate world cared much about their presence, unless, as was the case on Tetra Prime, those Red Listers were squatting on something of value.

According to the brief, the people of RLC5611 had settled on the planet for reasons unknown, but in the process of establishing their colony, had discovered micro-deposits of nefadrite ore in the scorched silt dunes that now covered the planet.

The colony had been positioned in this particular valley due to the prevailing wind patterns. With a series of massive turbines they churned through the wind to separate the nefadrite ore from the rest of the silt. When nefadrite began to appear on the black market several companies took interest, and investigators went to work tracking the ore back to its source.

A Helion investigator had found the link between the purchase of the turbines to the Red Listed colonists. Helion, much like Grotto, was a galaxy spanning mega-corporation with interests across the universe and the relationship between Helion and Grotto was somewhat poor at present.

Though every company in the universe was engaged in some manner of trade war with one or more opponents, most military engagements were clandestine and only rarely would formal war be declared. In fact, the last formal wars had been fought between Grotto, Aegis, and the now defunct Wageri corporations nearly a century prior.

In those hard years, entire cities were drawn into the conflict. Many administrators and educators insisted that now, war was a more civilized affair and violence only occurred on actual work sites and resource locations.

It was a convenient narrative to spin for the masses, thought Samuel as he looked down on the colony, some of its buildings still smoking from the Helion occupation.

When Helion battle forces stormed the settlement Samuel imagined that the colonists would disagree with the official corporate historians. According to available intelligence a sizeable Helion battle force had entered Grotto space and seized the colony roughly seventy-two hours prior.

Grotto Corporation had become aware of the nefadrite deposits and turbine colony thanks only to the invasion causing the Grotto investigators to finally put two and two together. The corporation was engaged in several mining and gas harvesting operations on other planets and moons in the Tetra Prime system and it was deemed an Alpha Priority to drive out the Helion invaders. Not just to push them out of a Grotto system in general, but also to protect the existing infrastructure of the colony so that once under Grotto control the nefadrite extraction could continue.

The rest of Squad Taggart was strapped into seats alongside Samuel. The new marine was Bianca Kade, and though she'd been with the squad for the last three years, having replaced the marine lost back on the space hulk, Samuel couldn't help but think of her as Aaron's replacement.

Aaron Baen had died back on M5597, sitting against a wall and forgotten by his comrades during the furious firefight. Samuel had always felt it was his fault that Aaron had been allowed to bleed out.

Plenty of other marines had insisted to Samuel that these sorts of things happened on the battlefield, that while Aaron lay bleeding Samuel was fighting for his own life.

Samuel knew this to be true, but he had not been able to shake that feeling of responsibility and guilt for years. Aaron was his first medic patient and the first casualty of Squad Taggart since the founding on Baen 6. Samuel had figured that was why he had so much trouble learning the names of Aaron's replacements. It wasn't until Bianca joined the squad that he'd finally gotten over it. Granted, Samuel had to admit to himself, that was likely also, in part, to he and Bianca having taken to each other's bed several times over the last few years.

The marine carried a great deal of guilt about his multiple infidelities since joining the Reapers. He knew that one day he had to come clean with Sura. He wondered how he could possibly communicate to her the raw need for human contact that rose up within him, within most all of the marines, when they survived a particularly harrowing engagement.

Samuel's first time had been with Jada after the fight with the monsters on M5597. As for Bianca, she'd come to him for comfort after the two of them had spent nearly an hour pinned down and exchanging sniper fire with a mob of armed squatters who refused to leave a decommissioned refinery during the Hive Fleet 822 campaign.

Samuel knew about plenty of other relationships and trysts within Tango Platoon and with other platoons. It was next to impossible to keep secrets on board the Reaper tug, and most people didn't even attempt to hide anything.

Each marine carried with them the burdens of their debts, some the responsibility for their families, and all of them the knowledge that each mission could be their last.

Only a small handful of marines in the Reaper ranks were without some family connection planetside, like Boss Marsters, so even in their infidelity, there was a common bond between the marines and their comrades.

As he thought of comrades, Samuel's gaze fell upon the other people in the combat speeder. In addition to Squad Taggart there were three elite troopers who perched in the on-board launch tubes. They were members of the *Folken*, a mercenary force contracted by Grotto to lead the assault on RLC5611.

While the Reapers were capable soldiers, they were not explicitly armed or trained for front line combat duty against Alpha class opposing forces. Reapers were qualified to engage

Charlie class enemies such as squatters and unclassified hostiles in addition to Beta class enemies such as space pirates.

Most corporate security forces were considered Alpha class enemies, along with elite troopers and armored divisions. The Helion battle force that had occupied the colony consisted of all three sorts of Alpha class threats.

Grotto had issued a rapid response contract to known merc units in the sector. Within forty-eight hours the *Folken* elites arrived along with their own small compliment of combat speeders and one especially intimidating battle tank. The three elites were wearing armored dropsuits, which in addition to being resistant to most small arms fire had built-in gravity dampeners that would allow them to break their fall from extreme heights.

The launch tubes in the combat speeder were designed to catapult the troopers into the air across enemy lines. With the gravity-dampeners, the elites could descend into the thick of the enemy position and be combat capable instantly.

Two of them were armed with what Samuel knew to be rail guns, very expensive and devastating weapons that fired high velocity projectiles capable of shredding most infantry armor.

The third warrior, a giant of a man who wore a much heavier dropsuit that was no doubt even more potently armored, carried a multi-barreled machine gun that made Ben Takeda's heavy gun look comically inadequate.

The faceplates on the helmets the two rail gunners were molded into masks that looked like snarling beasts of some kind, giving them an otherworldly look. The heavy gunner's face was obscured by a grinning maw of three dimensional teeth as well as having what looked to be horns grafted to the sides of his helmet.

One of the beast-masks turned his head to Samuel, as if he'd noticed the additional scrutiny, that or the sound of yet another approaching combat speeder. There were now three at the mouth of the ravine, each carrying three elites and a squad of Reapers from Tango Platoon.

The valley had several more such ravine entrances and other combat speeders were filling them as well, all careful to remain under cover and arriving one at a time to avoid warning the enemy of the impending assault. Once the attack had begun, a helo-craft would air drop the battle tank directly into the thick of the fighting, to further increase the shock factor and give the enemy something harder to shoot at while the lighter combat speeders delivered their soldiers into the fight.

The soldier returned Samuel's gaze for a moment, then his voice crackled through the com-bead in the marine's ear.

"You are, Reaper Hyst Samgir, of Platoon Tango, are you not?" asked the beast-mask, breaking the silence that had dominated the inside of the combat speeder ever since the two groups of soldiers joined each other inside.

"Roger, Samuel Hyst, REAPER, Platoon Tango," responded Samuel, keeping his tone formally neutral, as he was unsure of how to properly address an independent contractor.

The beast-mask inclined his head and said, "Forgive my speaking, Reaper Hyst Samgir, there are elements of your Grotto speech that are difficult to properly form with this Errolite tongue. I mean no offense."

Samuel involuntarily sucked in his breath at the realization that the mercenary was Errolite. The planet of Errol was nestled deep within Augur space, a corporation renowned for its technological advancements. Augur's chief exports were the multitudes of technological components that helped many of the machines in the universe operate.

While they did not hold a universe wide monopoly as a tech firm, they did control a large portion of business in the tech industry. Their secondary export was military units from the planet Errol. The Errolites were a tribal people, who, while having access to much of the contemporary technology of the age somehow still maintained a tribal society.

Errol was part of the Augur Corporation, though, unlike corporations such as Grotto or Helion that had somewhat homogenous internal cultures, the Augur Corporation consisted of many cultures. Augur's official stance was that multi-culturalism bred innovation. Though most other corporations disagreed with this sort of approach, the products created by Augur were of considerable quality and very advanced in nature, so their system seemed to work.

Augur's primary security forces were recruited from all across Augur space. Thanks to the warrior Errolite culture, the Augur military was staffed with many Errolite soldiers. They were too few to upset the balance of the universe by making Augur's military intrinsically stronger than other corporations, but the Errolite prowess in battle was common knowledge. Though most warriors of Errol fought under the Augur banner, there were some who still chose the life of an independent mercenary, contracting through the mercenary guild called the Merchants Militant. Such warriors fetched high prices, and from the stories told about them, it was apparent that they earned those wages.

Mag turned her head towards Samuel and kicked his boot, snapping Samuel out of his awe and reminding him of the present moment.

"No offense given," he replied sheepishly.

"Wargir, you must forgive Hyst for his curiosity, the Reapers are carrion birds, and we are not accustomed to front line duty, much less being in the presence of independent elites," said Mag in a voice heavy with formality. Samuel knew 'wargir' to be Errol slang for mercenary.

"Taggart Magir, if we are to fight and die together I would disperse the notion of your soldiers that we are anything but human beings underneath this armor, despite appearances to the contrary," said the wargir with a palpable mirth in his voice. "Our employers have determined that we elites inflict far too much collateral damage and must be given guidance by Reapers, so as to reign us in. To my thinking that makes us equals in this endeavor."

"Sounds good to me. I hate formalities anyway," said Mag as she leaned back in her seat. "These marines are a good bunch, just keep an eye on them while you're out there kicking ass, and you'll get an idea of what not to blast. We both know that things happen in the thick of the fight, and it's likely that the Reapers will fall behind your advance. So my advice is if it looks expensive, try to avoid destroying it."

"You are a very forward speaker, Taggart Magir, it is appreciated. Our employability rests in our ability to execute in accordance with our contractual specifications, so you may trust that we have been briefed on the technical elements of the mission, though as you've said, things happen in the midst of battle, and we are prepared to submit to your judgment should the occasion arise," spoke the wargir as he settled back into his launcher tube.

"Well, we're gonna get along just fine," said Mag as the warning klaxon rang and the lights in the speeder cabin went red to indicate that the assault was seconds from beginning, "Okay, marines, it's time to earn our hazard pay."

"This is the job!" called out five Reaper voices through the com-bead as the combat speeder engaged its thrusters.

Over a dozen combat speeders ignited, filling the valley with the roaring sound of their engines. Samuel could see below that the Helion forces had erected several mobile hardpoints that looked to be made of stacked drop-containers with hasty fighting positions dug into the ground so that infantry units could cover multiple angles.

The drop-containers had likely been ejected from a low orbit, made planetfall several miles away, then were recovered and brought back to the colony. Once emptied of their cargo, which likely consisted of an assortment of foodstuffs, ammunition, fuel, and building materials, the containers were utilized as the building blocks for defensive positions. Though Samuel had never seen such a thing in action, there had been several old battlefields the Reapers had scavenged over the years that contained such defenses among the decayed ruins.

Once the speeders were clear of the ravines they spread out in a loose formation to avoid being hammered by the mortar rounds that immediately began sailing towards them from behind the enemy positions.

The Grotto forces had not dared to fire mortars or rockets, much less employ air strikes, against the colony for fear of damaging the valuable hard assets. Helion undoubtedly knew this, and had drawn their forces into the colony itself to prevent their enemies from being able to employ bombardment tactics. Helion did have a battle tank visibly rolling down main street, but the Grotto forces would have to engage the armored war machine without the help of field artillery.

The *Folken* tank wasn't even part of the initial assault, from what Samuel had gathered, but was more of a deterrent against possible counter attacks in the event that Grotto pushed Helion out of the colony. Both Helion and Grotto forces knew that this fight was going to be an infantry brawl.

Samuel was impressed by the skill and bravado of the *Folken* combat speeder pilots as they threaded their way through the valley floor, using the dunes as partial cover against the fusillade of enemy fire. The bass crump of an explosion came from ahead of them on the right, and Samuel saw that a combat speeder had taken a direct hit from the mortars. The vehicle's left thruster had disintegrated and as the marine watched, the speeder began tumbling end over end as it bled flaming fuel and scrap metal. The elite troopers launched from their tubes, and while two of them sailed skyward, one was launched directly into a dune. Samuel wondered if the warrior's dropsuit would protect him from the impact or not, then was startled as the speeder finally exploded.

"That was Lamda Platoon," growled Mag, as their speeder left the wreckage behind and continued towards the target, "Reagan Ander's mob, good marines."

The rest of the Reapers remained silent, keenly aware that at any moment mortar fire could rip them to shreds just as easily. The speeder's turret guns coughed and sent semi-automatic stub rounds toward the enemy positions.

Stub rounds were low velocity, high mass rounds that were designed for maximum impact, but minimal penetration. The turret guns of all the speeders had been outfitted with stub rounds so that they could engage the enemy effectively without overly damaging any hard assets.

Samuel had noticed when he first boarded the speeder that each gun had a small reserve of armor piercing rounds in a backup magazine in case they engaged enemy armor. The stub rounds from several speeders raked the enemy gun emplacements and mortar stations, chewing apart the cheap flak-board that the Helion troops had erected to protect themselves from small arms fire.

The combat speeder was moving too quickly, changing directions every other second, making it difficult for Samuel to get an idea of how their approach was going. The constant barking of the turret gun overshadowed any other sounds while the hard banking of the speeder as they circled the colony, looking for a good place to launch the elites and then disgorge the marines, made hanging on a priority.

A small yellow light began blinking above each of the launch tubes and Samuel could see the three mercenaries make a final check of their tubes to make sure they were slotted in properly, and then they poised and waited.

"Luck in battle, comrades," said the wargir just before the yellow lights went solid and the tubes released, sending the three mercenaries upwards and out of sight.

Samuel and Patrick, the only ones seated so that they could see out of the viewports, watched for the elites, but they had been launched so high in the air that no visible sign of them could be found.

"They'll drop on Helion and give 'em a bloody nose don't you worry," said Mag as she rolled her shoulders and popped her neck. "Everybody get ready. As soon as the pilot finds an opening we're going to get dumped quick. Be ready to tuck and roll and come up shooting."

"Boss, is it a bad time to point out the fact that we've never trained for rapid combat insertion?" laughed Patrick as he looked around the cabin of the speeder, "That we haven't trained for any of this?"

Everyone, even Mag, laughed along with Patrick's gallows humor for a few moments, then the yellow lights above each of their seats began blinking. The marines went silent as each of them watched the lights. Samuel couldn't help but tap his boot in time with the light, as if counting out the rhythm to a song he could barely remember. Then the yellow lights went solid and a klaxon wailed as the combat speeder tilted slightly to the side. The hatch slid open in the blink of an eye and the straps holding the marines in place automatically retracted even as their seats turned and began catapulting them out of the hatch and onto the ground.

The combat speeder had thrown on its engine brakes and the back blast had retarded its forward momentum long enough for the five marines to be hurled to the ground.

Samuel did his best to land on his feet and then tuck his head and shoulder in so that he could roll the next several meters to slow his velocity. It worked for the first somersault and then he didn't quite stick the landing, ending up flailing into the dune helmet first. He scrambled to pull his head from the silt dune and recover his weapon, only to find that his combat rifle had flown from his hands and was easily two meters ahead of him. Rising to his feet, he sprinted towards his rifle as small arms fire erupted all around him. Samuel didn't dare look at anything but the rifle, knowing that the moment he witnessed the madness of the battle he would lose precious seconds in recovering his ability to participate and survive.

Hard rounds sent up plumes of silt as Samuel was fired upon and he began zigzagging as he ran before diving for his weapon. In a feat of dexterity that surprised him, he snatched the gun as he fell and managed to tuck his shoulder to the ground so that he somersaulted end over end as he twisted his body around. He came up from the roll facing the enemy with his combat rifle raised and began squeezing the trigger. Samuel's aim was true and he watched as a Helion trooper staggered backwards, falling off of a firing stoop of the barricade in a spray of blood and sparks.

Samuel finally dared to take a moment to assess the battle space and found that he was not the only marine to flub the landing. Ben was only now managing to get to his feet and shake the silt from his heavy gun as Patrick dug with his hands to unearth his fallen combat rifle. Mag and Bianca, however, were both in an aiming crouch and pouring on suppressing fire as the squad pulled itself together.

"Let's go marines! Push through! Push through!" bellowed Mag as she turned to see her people finally getting to their feet and preparing to engage.

Samuel and Patrick rushed past the two women and sprinted towards the sheer side of the barricade under cover of the suppressing fire.

Ben finally got his heavy gun up and spinning and was able to begin picking targets and shredding enemy positions while Bianca and Mag reloaded and rushed to join the vanguard. Once they joined Samuel and Patrick, the group penetrated the enemy line through the gaps that had been punched through the flak-board barricades that connected each of the container defenses. Ben kept up his high rate of fire as he began to advance, not wanting to get caught out in the open when he inevitably ran out of ammunition, which, at this speed would be very soon.

Samuel and Mag broke left while Patrick and Bianca broke right, each pair seeking to engage the defenders that held the container hardpoints. Samuel fired several rounds through the leg of a female Helion trooper who darted out and attempted to flank the marines and then Mag put a round through the woman's faceplate.

Rushing up the staircase behind the container as Mag covered him from below, the marine stopped just before the top of the stairs and pitched a frag grenade over his head. As expected, a cry of surprise went up from the defenders and one of them attempted to rush down the stairs, only to be riddled with bullets and fall over the side of the stairs as Samuel squeezed the trigger. The grenade exploded and sent pieces of at least one more trooper flying in multiple directions.

He low crawled to the top of the stairs just to make sure there weren't any troopers left. As he surveyed the grisly remains, he saw the wargir standing on the top of the next container over. The mercenary had slain the defenders and was hurling rail gun rounds into an alleyway that led into the colony. Return fire pinged off of his armor finally forcing him to leap off of the container to the ground. As Samuel watched the mercenary kept firing, charging into the alley and out of sight.

"Hyst, get back down here, we need to start taking and holding urban ground!" shouted Mag as she, Bianca, Patrick, and Ben converged on the alley that was nearest them. "We need to get in tight where we're comfortable. Reapers aren't meant for war on open ground."

Samuel hurried back down the stairs and joined the squad as Mag led them into the colony. They emerged from the alley to see the mercenary gunning down several more Helion troopers before leaping back into cover. More troopers began firing on him from behind a barricade they'd built to bisect the small colony's main street.

The barricade was made out of the burned out shells of what appeared to be civilian transport vehicles and irregular scraps of flak board that had been left from the primary wall construction. The marines emerged from the alley and began firing on the barricade. Mag hurled a frag grenade that rocked the barricade and displaced one of the vehicles enough that someone could fit through it.

The wargir had apparently noticed the gap because he began sprinting for it, much faster than humanely possible thanks to the servos in his dropsuit. The marines continued to give cover fire as the mercenary reached the gap and disappeared behind it. The whir of his rail gun could be heard as Mag gestured for Samuel and Bianca to back him up. The two marines leapt through the gap and saw that the mercenary had already shot down three of the troopers. His rail gun had finally gone dry, but instead of reloading, he slung it over his back and drew a pistol from his hip holster.

Bianca shouted and began firing at a trooper who was taking aim at Samuel from inside the window of a burned out hab-block, though before she could drill a hole in the trooper's throat with her bullet, the attacker managed to get a clean shot at Samuel. The marine went down spinning as the round struck his helmet. The only reason it didn't core his skull was that Bianca's scream had made him turn at the last instant. Thanks to that, what would have been a direct kill shot had become a glancing blow. Samuel blacked out for a few seconds, but came to as he saw Bianca standing over him, continuing to fire at other targets. He could hear the bark of the wargir's pistol and got shakily to his feet as the marine and the mercenary finished off the enemies in their immediate area.

"Let's get some height! Samuel and Ben take that hab-block and get me eyes on the rest of this colony!" ordered Mag as she and the rest of the squad came through the gap. "Patrick and Bianca on me. We're going to make sure nobody comes up behind our boys."

Samuel and Ben rushed towards the hab-block only to be beaten there by the wargir, now carrying his freshly reloaded rail gun. The wargir took point and blasted a trooper who had been hiding in the ruins, apparently afraid to join in the fighting, but unable to escape.

Samuel was taken aback for a moment at how swiftly and effortlessly the mercenary had eliminated the man. It was likely any one of the mercenaries would have done the same. The speed at which the merc weighed the man's life was astonishing. The wargir took more small arms fire as he reached the second floor, and with Samuel's help the two of them gunned down another trooper who looked to have been attempting to assemble a mortar launcher.

The two marines and the elite managed to reach the top of the four-story building without any additional resistance. As they took up observation positions on the rooftop they were indeed able to see the unfolding battle as a complete tableau. The combat speeders still circled the colony, though they had, for the most part, ceased firing on the enemy positions, as they were now mostly overrun.

The Helion battle tank was a smoking wreck, apparently torn apart by a series of explosive devices placed across its side. There was some fighting in the streets as marines and elites moved through the colony, though not nearly as much resistance as Samuel would have thought. From the look on Ben's face it seemed as if he agreed.

"Something is not right," muttered the wargir as he tapped his com-bead, "This should have been a harder fight."

Samuel could see the wreckage of one other combat speeder and wondered if it had disgorged its soldiers before being shot down. Through the smoke and dust it did seem as if the assault smashed the defenses and routed the enemy much more swiftly and with fewer casualties than he would have imagined. That was when Ben tapped on Samuel's shoulder and pointed. The wargir and the marines looked out as explosions of sand and dust shot skyward across the valley floor. Helion elite troopers, positioned in portable launch tubes buried in the sand dunes surrounding the colony burst from their hiding places and began firing on the Grotto forces as they sailed through the air. As the elites arched towards the colony, groups of Helion troopers erupted from within several of the, as yet, uncontested buildings and began retaking the colony.

Because the Grotto forces were thinly spread out and still heavily engaged across the colony, the Helion forces superior numbers and firepower turned what had seemed like an easy victory into an all-out melee in a matter of moments.

The wargir shouted a battle cry and took up a firing position that allowed him to spray rail rounds into an advancing squad of Helion troopers, managing to put three on the ground before their return fire drove him back into cover.

Ben rushed to the far right side of the wargir's position to open up on the squad, felling another as the last trooper was driven into the first floor of the very building the marines held. More shooting came from inside and Samuel was positive that Mag and the others had eliminated the last trooper.

Samuel could see that as the Helion elites used their gravity dampeners to make landfall, the Grotto elites moved to intercept them on the other side of the barricades. The elites ripped into each other like armored titans as they ignored the marines and troopers around them, the lesser soldiers suddenly insignificant compared to the epic conflict of the elites.

Samuel reloaded his spent magazine and watched as the elites warred against each other, one peerless warrior finally pitted against worthy opponent.

The troopers and marines steered clear of the elite engagements on open ground and found themselves being drawn into more conventional firefights in the tight confines of the colony.

Three Helion elites made landfall near the hab-block, one on the roof adjacent and the others in the street below. Samuel saw the wargir with the horned helmet standing out in the open on the main street firing his heavy gun and tearing apart one of the enemy elites who landed in the street before being fragged himself by fire from the elite on the rooftop.

The mercenary that stood with Samuel leapt across the alleyway as he fired and by the time he landed on the adjacent building the enemy elite was a rent corpse. The wargir began firing at another target on the other side of the building that the marine couldn't see. When gunfire erupted downstairs, Samuel left the wargir to his fate and rushed to the levels below. As Samuel raced downstairs Ben continued to fire at more Helion troopers from the rooftop, doing his best to keep the hab-block from being overrun.

As the gunfire continued and Samuel finally reached the first floor, he was met with a savage engagement. Patrick was crouched behind a row of bullet riddled laundry machines as he exchanged fire with two Helion troopers. The body of a third lay midway between them and the marine's position.

The armored body of the Helion elite who had escaped the horned wargir's barrage was laying in the middle of the room bleeding from what must have been a tremendous amount of concentrated fire.

Bianca was bleeding from two ragged holes in her chest armor, but was heroically dragging Mag into cover. Samuel raised his rifle to his shoulder and emptied his magazine with disciplined precision as he walked down the remaining stairs one methodical step at a time. His first several rounds put a Helion trooper dead on the ground as more fire pushed the last trooper from his cover, then combined shots from Patrick and Samuel finished him off.

Samuel reloaded his combat rifle with detachment as his mind worked furiously to comprehend what he was seeing. He slung his rifle and said, "Patrick, you take over watch, I've got Kade."

Samuel leaned over Mag and began working swiftly to address Bianca's wounds. His med-kit appeared in his hands and he worked with a speed and precision that he'd never experienced before. He continued not looking at Mag and focused on his work as he spoke.

"When your heavy runs dry, Takeda, fall back to our first floor position," he said as he dosed Bianca with the stim cocktail, removed the marine's chest plate, and began addressing the ragged holes in her body, "There's a rail rifle down there, take possession and you'll still be effective as our heavy. We're moving in five."

Both marines tapped their com-beads in silent affirmation and Samuel finished his work on Bianca. The marine leaned against the wall and held her combat rifle across her lap as Samuel stood up and finally willed himself to look down at Mag.

The veteran's body was a bloody mess, having been shredded by a flurry of projectiles from the Helion elite's rail gun. It was likely that Bianca was in such a state of shock from being shot that she didn't realize she was dragging a corpse to safety.

Ben pounded down the stairs, his empty heavy gun slung across his back, and stopped just short of the bottom when he saw Mag's body. He and Samuel looked at each other for a silent moment before Ben nodded and walked over to the armored corpse of the Helion elite. As Ben stripped the rail gun from the elite's dead hands and began to collect the projectile drums, Patrick set about looting the bodies of the other Helion troopers. Samuel recovered a single magazine from Mag's body, which he slid into one of the empty holders on his thigh mount.

"That's odd," Patrick commented, "The ammunition on these Helion jokers is the same mil-spec as ours," He ejected a magazine from one of the enemy rifles and investigated the bullet, "Oh, wow, even the same manufacturer, Fenrir Industries, just like us."

"Why am I not surprised?" grumbled Ben as he stood up, continuing to tinker with the fittings on the gun, mimicking the movements he'd seen the wargir use to slot in the fresh projectile drum and prime it for firing.

"It makes sense, Fenrir Industries has no known interests in this system, even in this sector," said Samuel in a low voice as he scanned the streets for enemy troopers, all of whom seemed to, thankfully, be engaged elsewhere in the colony, "So they'd see no conflict of interests in selling ammunition to both Helion and Grotto. It would just be another transaction in their books."

"That's grim, man," said Ben as he joined Samuel in looking out into the street, "So what's the plan, Boss?"

At the unexpected designation Samuel looked at Ben. The heavy gunner pointedly continued to look out at the street. Samuel looked back at Patrick, who stood on the other end of the small room. He nodded at Samuel as he chambered a round in his combat rifle. Samuel took a deep breath and leaned down to help Bianca to her feet, bracing her on his shoulder as she did her best to hold onto her combat rifle with her off hand.

"When I was on the roof I saw one of the wargirs, the one with the mini-gun, walking past what looked like a Helion machine gun nest. He'd already wasted everybody in it, but from where I was standing it looked stout, better than staying here," Samuel said as he started moving toward the shattered back door of the hab-block. "It's a hardpoint, with several guarded fields of fire and it gets us back into the fight."

"Sounds good to me, Boss," confirmed Patrick as he leaned out to quickly check the alleyway, then gave the all-clear signal, "I'll take point."

Patrick ducked out of the doorframe and into the alley, immediately putting his back to the wall of the opposite building so that he could sweep his rifle across both ends of the alley. The marine saw no sign of the enemy and signaled to his team that he was moving onwards.

Patrick double-timed it down the alley before skidding to a halt at the mouth of the next gap in the buildings. He noticed a squad of Helion troopers rushing past them on the street going in the other direction. At first he thought they were perhaps gearing up to assault the hab-block that Squad Taggart had been holding, but as the last trooper crossed his field of vision he saw the trooper turn and fire several rounds behind him before continuing on.

Samuel, Bianca, and Ben joined Patrick and they continued onwards, finally stacking up at the mouth of a small side street that opened up to face the gun nest. They were near the edge of the colony and could still hear the sounds of furious combat and the roar of speeders exploding through the valley.

"Patrick, hold here with Bianca," said Samuel as he peered into the street to see that a group of Helion elites and troopers had occupied a squad building near the gun nest.

In the time since Samuel had seen the wargir slaughter the troopers in the nest, it looked as if another squad had taken the position. The two enemy positions were engaging a group of Reapers and at least one of the *Folken* elites in a shootout. It wasn't looking good for the Grotto forces.

They had been pinned down between the burning wreckage of a combat speeder and the pulverized remnants of the original Helion perimeter wall. If the Helion forces managed to hold the building for much longer the rest of their forces would rally around them and possibly push the Grotto forces out of the colony. If they got pushed back into the open it would be a shooting gallery. Samuel could see that while plenty of combat speeders still circled the town, most of them had expended their onboard ammunition and had been reduced to simple transport vehicles until they had a chance to re-supply.

"Ben, we've got to rush the nest," said Samuel darkly as he turned to face his friend, "If we can take the position fast enough we can possibly get in a few good hits before the troops in the building realize we've flanked them. Might help our guys push back and get a better fighting position."

"Son of a bitch, Prybar, when you decide to step up you really go for it!" laughed Ben. He rotated his shoulder in expectation of the coming violence, "Lead the way, boss."

Samuel observed their objective for a few seconds more, then gathered his legs underneath him and started sprinting towards the nest. The enemy had been using the mounted machine gun to keep the Grotto forces pinned down while their flanks were punished by the Helion forces in the building. Samuel knew that more Reapers were dying the longer he waited, but if he and Ben were shot down in a foolish charge it would serve no purpose.

When the Helion trooper operating the mounted weapon had to stop to reload, Samuel made his move. The two marines made a mad dash across the street, holding their fire until they were very near point blank range. Samuel's attention was focused on the machine gunner, the Helion trooper going down with holes shot through his back as Samuel approached. Ben's rail gun whirred and vomited projectiles in a deadly cloud that enveloped the troopers who occupied the nest. Samuel slung his rifle as he ran and vaulted the wall of the nest, trusting that his comrade marine would not only finish off the enemy, but also avoid shredding Samuel in the process. The marine knew that he had to turn the mounted gun on the building as soon as he could before the other Helion force knew what was coming.

Samuel landed as gracefully as he could and reached for the gun to steady himself as he stumbled. As it turned out, the stumble saved his life. A wounded, but still capable, Helion trooper raised a pistol and fired several rounds into the space where Samuel had been only milliseconds before.

Samuel whirled the heavy gun around even as he prayed that the previous operator had chambered the belt fed rounds. His luck held as he squeezed the trigger and the heavy gun belched a salvo of high velocity rounds tearing his adversary to pieces. Samuel then turned the gun on the handful of troopers who had survived Ben's fusillade and the machine gun turned them into bloody pulp.

Without pausing to release the trigger, Samuel brought the gun up and strafed the adjacent building occupied by the Helion troopers and elites. He found that he was screaming as the rounds blew apart one of the elites and several of the troopers before the belt ended and the gun clicked empty once more. Both Samuel and Ben dove for cover as they scrambled to reload their own weapons.

The marine's bold move had been noticed by the Grotto forces, and the Reapers took the opportunity to charge the Helion position while the enemy was reeling from the surprise attack. As Samuel and Ben lent their semi-automatic fire in support of the brazen charge the marines could see that the wargir who had been in their combat speeder was with the group.

The Helion forces were routed in short order, only to be cut down by more Reaper squads moving up from within the colony, having taken the interior with vicious street to street fighting spearheaded by the Folken elites.

Mere minutes after the death of Maggie Taggart, the squad rallied at the machine gun nest and held the position as Grotto

Reapers and *Folken* elites eliminated the last of the Helion defenders.

POINTS OF VIEW

Samuel had stabilized Bianca and sent up the call for a casualty recovery when he noticed the wargir sitting on the smoking hull of the Helion battle tank that had died just at the top of a nearby hill.

The wargir waved an invitation to Samuel and the marine trudged up the dune hill to join the mercenary in surveying the battlefield. The fighting was all but finished, and for the first time that day Samuel began to feel confident about the mission.

"Well, uh," Samuel wracked his brain for the other man's name. Imago. " Imago. Looks like we won," said Samuel off handedly as he sat down next to the mercenary, "Good day for Grotto and bad day for Helion. Can't say it feels all that victorious though, a lot of bodies out there that belong to us."

"Hyst Samgir," the mercenary said, "you must understand that when war is stripped of ideology, all that remains is the simple reality that it is nothing more, and nothing less, than the violent redistribution of wealth." He cocked his head at Samuel as they sat perched upon the burned out hull of a Helion battle tank. "Anyone who says differently is just trying to lower your pay rate."

The Errolite mercenary seemed to find humor in his own statement, and chuckled to himself behind his armored mask, which Samuel found particularly unsettling. They remained in silence for a moment, watching as the strange two headed birds of the tundra planet, which according to the fauna/flora briefing were a carrion species called kyracks, began to circle over the ravaged colony that lay smoldering in the valley below. The wargir gestured at the bloody chaos around them with a gauntleted hand.

"To anyone but those who fought and died here, this colony is just a name and a number, perhaps merely a number, in a vast accounting system that tallies inventory, personnel, property holdings, and monetary liquidity.

No matter how peaceful or neutral those who once lived here may have been, their resources were deemed worth the minimal cost for Helion forces to conquer and occupy this place.

Red Listed communities have no rights in the corporate world, and even that world is an illusion, it is the one we all fight for, the one that we, at present, ascribe to. A community with no rights cannot rely on anyone but themselves to protect it, because it exists outside of the system.

Captain Volk determined from our initial recon that the community did, at some point, have a small militia protecting it. Little evidence remains of them, just a few blasted gun nests and a half-slagged mech-warrior that looks to have been older than the colony itself. It must have been a feat of engineering for the colonists to keep it battle ready at all; much good it did them. Helion rolled over their petty militia in a matter of minutes, if our recon was accurate," Imago said, his voice monotone thanks to the helmet's modulator, "My point is, that someone, far away and privy to a broader scope of events in the universe than we, determined that this colony was worth taking. Then when this sector became contested space, those same people, or their successors, deemed it of continued interest to the Bottom Line that the colony remain in their possession. On our side, someone else determined that the colony, and the corresponding resources and projected revenues it represents, was worth the cost of assaulting."

"You're reducing this whole thing to money, like the bloody hell we just walked through was tantamount to a financial wager between two companies," argued Samuel, suddenly offended that the strange mercenary's callous logic reduced the life and death of Boss Maggie Taggart to the cost of doing business. "Like this whole thing is just a balance sheet on some administrator's desk."

The wargir's body registered surprise. "Isn't it? The events of today are logged, a tally taken of what was expended and what was gained," he said, "who lived and who died." He turned his grim visage to face Samuel.

"Eventually that log is turned into a report, which is sent through various chains of command, all the way to the unseen few who manage the Bottom Line. To them, the face-less masters of the universe, the deeds of our lives, be they glorious or vile, are merely data points on a balance sheet."

"Good people died down there today! Some of them were my friends!" Samuel snapped through gritted teeth. "Your unit didn't make it through unscathed either! I saw the man with the horns get blown to pieces!" He wasn't sure why he said it. It felt like retaliation for the mercenaries' previous remarks.

The Errolite mercenary considered Samuel for a moment from behind his wicked mask. The salvage marine held his gaze, not wanting to back down regardless of how fearsome the man was.

Something in the mercenary's posture changed and he nodded his head. Reaching up, he unfastened the pressure seals on his dropsuit helmet. After the airflow balanced out he lifted it from his head. For the first time since meeting the strange warrior that morning Samuel saw his actual human face.

Imago had dark brown eyes that matched his skin, though the entire left side of his face was a patchwork of tiny scars, while the right had a serrated looking spiral tattoo that started at his tear duct and curled down his cheek to end at his chin. The mercenary smiled to reveal canines filed to points.

"You misunderstand my meaning, Hyst Samgir, but you are a man of Grotto, so I understand that my words are strange. I show you my face so that you may know me as friend." His expression softened and he looked once more out over the colony as the birds squawked and descended to feast upon the dead for as long as they could before the salvage marines shooed them away, "When the *Folken* go to war it is because we have accepted a contract and are being paid to fight. There is no ideology at work in our hearts or minds, but a simple contract to be executed.

Those who live and die by the sword, those like you and I, Hyst Samgir, would die of heartbreak sooner than violence were we to attempt to place value judgments on the righteousness of one war over another. The *Folken* have seen this truth, and it armors us against the decay of mind, body, and spirit that plagues all men and women who go to war. We sleep very well at night, my friend, because there is no cause upon which we judge ourselves, only that we were paid and the contract fulfilled.

We rise to make ourselves equals to those who watch the Bottom Line by creating our own and fighting like devils for it." Imago growled with obvious pride. "This is a hard universe, and the grim tide of war ever rises and ebbs upon the shores of everyone's life. Even those who never see a battlefield are forever affected by it. Those balance sheets, the Bottom Line, is part of everyone's life, and has been since humanity first took up sticks and stones."

Samuel studied the peaceful face before him, no anger, guilt or loss was reflected upon the placid visage.

"When you speak of it like that, there is a poetry to it all, Imago, and thanks for sharing. I mean no offense when I say this," Samuel nodded to the mercenary in acknowledgement, "But I still do not see the blood and dirt and individual life in your philosophy. I don't see the man in the horned helmet, or my friends. It all sounds pretty textbook, like you've memorized this speech in front of a mirror over and over until you got it perfect."

Imago nodded his head. He reached into his satchel to produce a slagged piece of helmet that that bore the unmistakable base of one of the horns from the helmet worn by the elite Samuel had seen cut down. Imago stood, and turned the piece over and over in his hands. He looked back at Samuel.

"The men and women who ride with the *Folken* are from many worlds, many cultures, but we when we fight we do so as one people, one tribe. The money is what determines when and where we fight, but once battle is joined, it is our comrades and our families that keep us striving for victory and survival." Imago's eyes suddenly moistened with emotion. "When the armor comes off, we are all just human beings. This is why I show you my face to speak with you thusly."

Samuel watched without comment as Imago turned his attention back to the helmet fragment.

"His name was Costa Sagge. He was a veteran of many campaigns, the father of three children, the husband of two. He lived on a ship that perpetually sailed the oceans of Abzu," Imago's voice was solemn and grave, as if reciting an epitaph. He lifted the jagged remnant to his lips and kissed the top of it gently. "His tithe is paid."

Imago placed the helmet fragment back into his satchel with a degree of finality and turned to face Samuel.

"As you know, the Merchants Militant maintain strict confidentiality when negotiating and executing contracts so that there is little to no direct contact between mercenary operators and corporate employers," said Imago as he reached into a compartment in his armor withdraw two small data-coins with a symbol embossed on the surface that looked like a skull with a rifle and sword on either side of it.

"Makes sense, given that you sell your services to whoever can afford your rates," Samuel replied. "I could see it being easy to make enemies out there. Grotto, at least, provides us with some sense of place, an idea of whose side we're on." Samuel's voice was flat, devoid of the confidence in his words he might have felt just a few years ago. "Without the shelter of the corporate umbrella, we're on our own and no better than the Red List."

"This is the purpose of the Merchants Militant; it provides us with shelter, of a sort. Though we belong to no corporation or even hail from similar cultures, all registered mercenaries have a reasonable expectation of privacy," Imago replied. "We arrive, we fight, we get paid, and we leave. There is a simplicity to that which is a shelter all its own."

The mercenary then returned his helmet to his head and stood up. He tapped a locator beacon on his forearm and almost immediately one of the combat speeders approached the hill.

"Most of us live in the more remote places of the universe," Imago said, "where we can use our wealth as a shield against corporate interests, to keep our homes wild, our hearts free and our families healthy," The speeder pulled up near the hill and a hatch opened, revealing several other elites and an empty seat within.

"You don't worry about being on the frontier? Even Abzu is on the edge of a pretty wild tract of unmapped space," questioned Samuel as he stood politely to see Imago off.

The mercenary considered Samuel's comment for a moment, then nodded towards the battlefield below them as he said,

"A philosopher and an economist might speak in agreement that they see the view below to represent both the best and the worst aspects of capitalism. What I see is truth. Two great houses competing for resources, their economic struggle expressed as a military conflict, and crushed between them are the Red Listed colonists.

They probably thought they were lucky to have discovered such a valuable resource, that is, before the tanks and the soldiers. To exist outside the system, but still be subject to its power, is a desperate sort of freedom. The *Folken* are still part of the system, though we live upon its fringes."

Samuel frowned. "So you're saying the only difference between your people and the Red Listed is the fact that you still fight for the system, even if you loathe it and keep yourself and your families apart from it," he snorted. "It doesn't seem like you hold civilization in much high regard."

"There is time enough for civilization when we are at war," replied Imago. "As long as we are willing to pay the tithe when our times comes, it is a good life." Imago offered Samuel the data-coins. "Hyst Samgir, each day as a soldier you risk your life. The wise man gets paid as much as he can, as fast as he can, so that he may retire before the tithe takes him.

Your deeds on the field were noticed by the *Folken* and we agree that you and your comrade Takeda Bengir have earned these. A coin for each of you, and once a second is earned, upon any field and by the hand of any wargir, you will be able to seek membership to the Merchants Militant. I hope that one day soon there will be a place for you among us." He gave Samuel a firm warrior's handshake. "Until that day."

The mercenary nodded once to Samuel, then boarded the vehicle without another word. As the speeder rocketed out of sight Samuel could see that many other speeders and various planetside ships were leaving the area en masse.

Now that the hardest of the fighting was done the elite troopers were pulling out. It was the duty of the Reapers to mop up the last pockets of resistance, strip the dead, and begin the clean up and salvage operation. It was the battlefield clean up phase of the process that seemed to tug at Samuel's resolve the hardest. It was one thing to fight and survive in the furious chaos of battle, but once the combat was over, Samuel found that the violence did not stop. There were corpses, both enemy and comrade, to be looted, cataloged, and incinerated. There would be a multitude of fires to extinguish and untold chemical spills, fuel leaks, and containment breaches.

The Reaper environmental suit was of a very old make and model. Though they were ugly to behold, they were indeed robust in their effectiveness. Over the last four years Samuel had endured a broad range of hazardous materials during the clean up phase of the salvage operation. This colony operation did have its differences however, as this was the first battle in which the salvage marines had been part of a front line action.

Reapers were much like the kyracks, Samuel mused as he watched the flights of birds dart in and out of the battlefield while marines moved through the area. The salvage marines were deployed to the abandoned places of the universe, the decommissioned, the derelict, and the forgotten, to pick over the bones of the remains in the aftermath of battle. It was somewhat out of their scope to be placed on the front line of a trade war. While Reapers were indeed soldiers, they were predominantly salvage workers who had military training and hardware. Their combat effectiveness on the front line paled in comparison to the likes of Imago and his comrades.

Samuel walked down the hill as he thought of Mag. It was she, among many other Reapers, who had paid the price today for the administration's insistence that a salvage team participate. When Samuel looked at the conflict in the terms laid out by Imago's grim philosophy, it made perfect sense to have the Reapers present, as they, unlike the elite troopers, were trained to fight in such a way as to preserve the mission target. For the salvage marines, the purpose of any given mission was asset procurement or recovery. The marines used small caliber weapons, few explosives, and were trained to avoid causing unwarranted collateral damage.

Elite troopers had little concern for such things, and were more likely to destroy anything in their path rather than concern themselves with preserving buildings, hardware, or potential resources. In time, Mag would simply be logged in the loss category, and her life would be balanced against the net gains made by the corporation.

PROFIT AND LOSS

Samuel looked out over the battlefield, feeling as if he was seeing it with new eyes indeed. Many of the buildings had been spared destruction, as had most of the vespine gas reserves. The Helion forces were so soundly beaten that they'd left behind much of their own military and mining hardware, which would no doubt be considered an additional gain allocation on the final operation balance sheet.

When he looked at it from the perspective of the Bottom Line, Samuel could see that this had shaped up to be a very profitable venture and that the lives of the marines lost today would be considered a worthwhile expenditure in the course of conducting business in the sector. This battle was going to make an administrator's career, thought Samuel as he watched the first of the Reaper breaker skiffs hitting atmosphere.

Samuel walked down the hill to join Ben and Patrick, who had been resting in the shade of a blasted out storefront near the edge of town, just beneath the hilltop. They had taken their helmets off, which was generally frowned upon as a breach of military discipline, especially since the fighting had not ended officially.

"Hyst, pull your squad together and converge on my waypoint. I'm uploading to your man's rig now," crackled the deep voice of Boss Marsters in Samuel's com-bead. "There's a problem with the turbines down there. Looks like a few hostiles got left behind when Helion pulled out. Double time it marines!"

"Takeda! Patrick! Get your helmets on!" shouted Samuel as he strode towards them, "We're back online."

Ben and Patrick appeared taken aback by Samuel's commanding tone, though they did as they were told and donned their helmets. Ben left his heavy machine gun where it sat and hefted a Helion rail rifle.

Though it wasn't protocol to use off-brand weapons, without the chance for a rest and refit, the marines used whatever tools they could to suit the job at hand. From what Samuel could see Ben had managed to figure out how to operate the rail rifle, no doubt from watching Imago and Costa Sagge.

"I've got the waypoint, looks like we're only a few clicks away," said Patrick as he started off at a run, followed by Samuel and Ben.

As they sprinted through the colony streets, Samuel was reminded of the brutal combat that had occurred there only hours before. Where there had once been a furious storm of smoke, gunfire, blood, and the roar of tank engines, now the streets were bustling with the busy work of salvage and repair. Samuel figured that if the pace of work stayed consistent, the colony would be cleaned up and back to optimal production within a few days. After a few weeks it would be as if there was no battle here at all.

Boss Marsters was waiting with his squad at the entrance to the turbine station. The squad leader nodded at Samuel and gave the signal to move out.

"Squad Ulanti is already inside, they're pinned down by an unknown number of shooters. They'd send elites in there to root them out with seeker rounds, but the turbines are necessary for the vespine extraction," said Boss Marsters as the two squads descended the stairs to the sound of sporadic gunfire from within the station, "We need to flank whoever is down there and get this fight finished without damaging the turbines."

"Grotto can't just buy some replacements? This colony is a big win, they're gonna be swimming in cash once this place gets liquidated," protested Ben as they crept through the half-light of the station, moving slowly down a series of hallways and empty monitoring rooms.

"The administrators want this place back up to full production as soon as possible, they're only going to liquidate the salvaged Helion assets," Boss Marsters replied as he continued onward. "Replacement turbines would delay the whole project by months."

"We're the cheaper option, brother," said Samuel as he took point position from Ben, since his combat rifle was better suited to the close quarters gloom of the station.

The sound of gunfire continued to ring out, and finally Samuel was able to reach the end of the maze of halls and engineer compartments as the walkway opened up to reveal the primary turbine chambers.

From his vantage point, Samuel could see that Squad Ulanti had entered the building through the access tunnels in an attempt to infiltrate the building from the lowest point and clear their way upwards as was standard Reaper tactic. However, it appeared as if something had slowed their progress. They were holding position beneath a gigantic sump-water tank that was already riddled with bullet holes and leaking gallons of pressurized water across the base of the station. As he tried to get a clue as to what had them pinned down a whirring sound came from below as Samuel was joined by Ben and the rest of the marines.

"Mini-gun!" shouted Boss Marsters as he pushed Samuel and Ben to the side, shoving Jada back into the walkway, "Scatter!"

From somewhere below the weapon began spitting rounds at the newly arrived marines and the two old friends from Baen scampered to avoid being pulped by the salvo. The marines hurled themselves down the corrugated metal stairwell, tumbling a full flight down to the next level, well ahead of the bullets that chased them.

Samuel was dazed, but pushed himself to his feet and raised his combat rifle just in time to see a mech-warrior painted in Helion logos switching off its mini-gun and rotating the weapon arm to activate what appeared to be an infantry sized plasma-lance.

Ben roared and began firing his rail gun as he and Samuel rushed to get out of the enemy's line of fire. Their only hope was to keep moving and use their superior mobility to out-flank the mech-warrior. The two marines had landed on the wrong side of the water container and were unable to use it for cover, so they ran past it, doing their best to dodge the high-pressure spray of the water as it poured from the rents in the container.

Ben's rail-gun slammed enough bullets into the mech-warrior that it finally stumbled and was forced to readjust its aim as Samuel continued to cut to the right while Ben lunged left laying down suppressing fire. By then the rest of the marines above had begun to pour fire down on top of it.

The mech's armor was strong, though enough projectiles slammed into it that the odd round was managing to damage the robust war machine. Ben's weapon clicked empty and he kneeled behind cover to slot a fresh magazine, which seemed to be giving him some trouble, as the weapon, though powerful, was still unfamiliar. The mech-warrior's off hand was outfitted with a basic combat rifle attachment, drum fed for continuous use, and the mech-warrior sprayed semi-automatic fire at the marines above as it turned the plasma-lance towards Samuel.

The marine had hoped to skirt the edge of the container and work his way around behind the mech-warrior, but as the plasma-lance fired, his world became one of steam and pain. The lance fired its bolt of super-heated plasma at the decking instead of the marine. The incredible heat from the shot had instantly turned hundreds of gallons of standing water and what still poured out of the container, into steam that expanded outwards like an explosion.

Samuel was knocked off of his feet by a surge of lethal steam that sent him into convulsions of pain. His Reaper environmental suit had kept him alive, even though many of the seams in the armor had been heated sufficiently to burn his skin. The marine blinked through the pain and did his best to scamper the rest of the way around the corner to get one of the massive turbines between him and the mechanized enemy.

Through the shouts and gunfire he could make out the voice of Lucinda Ulanti and Wynn Marsters in his com-bead shouting orders. He realized that the pinned down squad had used the steam explosion as a cover for maneuvering into a better position. The marines were engaging the mech-warrior from both sides. Now that the enemy was using a plasma-lance, the chance of damaging the turbines was dramatically high.

Samuel reached into his med-kit and snatched a stimulant vial, slotting it into his hypo and dosing himself into full alertness.

He knew he was playing a dangerous game with the drugs, as the stim boost would only last for a few minutes before it began to slow his system down. The shot was designed to keep the victim from going into shock before gently easing them into unconsciousness.

Samuel got to his feet and began searching for a way to engage the mech. While the small arms fire from the marines would keep it busy, it was doubtful that they would be lucky enough to score a direct hit on the warrior's weak-points before the war machine was able to inflict significant casualties. It was a miracle that Squad Ulanti was still at full strength. As Samuel took a moment to survey the battlefield, he could see that another squad of salvage marines, from what platoon he couldn't tell in the gloom, had been killed to the last marine. They must have been the ones to send up the emergency call in the first place.

In all likelihood, the mech-warrior had fled the battle when the tide took a hard turn against Helion. When the enemy corporate forces had decided to back out of the fight, their various ships, tanks, and speeders had made their exits so swiftly that several pockets of enemy troops and vehicles were left behind by their comrades in the chaos. This mech-warrior was likely engaged against elites and was driven inside the turbine station, though once such a highly prized piece of salvage was in play the elites were pulled away from the engagement to be replaced by Reapers. Samuel gritted his teeth and silently raged at the callous indifference of the administration as he realized that the shift manager, or her superior, had made the decision to send in salvage marines, who carried no anti-armor weapons or demolitions, to engage the mech-warrior that they knew was inside. If management had sent in elites, who were equipped to deal with that class of hostile, then blame for the damaged turbines would fall squarely upon management. However, if the shift manager or her superior followed protocol, even though it flew in the face of real world events on the battlefield, and sent in the salvage marines, then there would be no blame to bear.

Samuel nodded his head grimly as he realized that management knew that the turbines were unlikely to escape this battle undamaged, but because they followed the rules of engagement their jobs would be secure. The balance sheet might have had a smaller profit margin for the loss of the turbines, but the report would be much cleaner and easier to file seamlessly without the black mark of allocated collateral damage.

If the salvage marines were sent to deal with the mech-warrior then the damage to the turbines would be written off as standard battle hazard, and all because of the way the conflict would look on the after-action report. Nowhere in any of those calculations would there be the consideration for the lives of the marines who were knowingly marched into that deathtrap by their leaders.

Imago's words rattled around inside Samuel's head as he crept towards the mech-warrior while it exchanged salvos with the marines who were now scattered around the station. It was all about the money, until you were in the fight, and then it was about your comrades, recalled Samuel as he watched his friends fighting hard against a superior foe.

The lights in the station were on emergency levels only, so much of the station was bathed in a murky darkness, temporarily lit by muzzle flashes and tracer fire as the combatants fought. It was in that moment that Samuel decided to let Grotto's apparent policy of indifference work for him and his comrades.

"Tango Platoon, listen up!" Samuel shouted into his com-bead as he crawled up the service ladder of the turbine he'd been hiding behind. "I'm tracking critical turbine damage to Unit 12 and Unit 17 from gunfire, and the whole D Block looks like it might have shorted out after the hydro-container breach."

"Prybar, I'm not seeing anything wrong on Unit 17," responded Boss Ulanti from somewhere in the gloom. "What's your position? What are you seeing?"

"I'm above it all, and I see everything," replied Samuel, his voice taking a low tone of authority that surprised himself and the others, "The turbines are lost, so instead of getting killed trying to protect damaged goods, let's get this fight over with."

"Hyst, our mission is to preserve the turbines and from here I don't see that any have been damaged!" snapped Boss Ulanti. "You're stepping out of rank, soldier."

"Lucinda, I'm seeing the problem too, Prybar is right, this place is lost," piped up Boss Marsters from his vantage point at the top of the walkway. "We can use the turbines for cover once they are reclassified as scrap."

"I don't see anything, but it's your call, Marsters," snarled Boss Ulanti over the com-bead. "If management wants to hang someone out to dry, it won't be me."

"Copy that, Ulanti," said Boss Marsters in a flat tone, and then he shouted, "Tango Platoon, you are now officially in a weapons free environment! Take cover when and where you choose. Stay scattered and draw his fire, eventually this guy is going to run out of ammunition, so all we have to do is keep him gunning without getting pasted."

Now that they were free to engage the mech-warrior through the turbine columns the salvage marines had much more access to hard cover, in addition to better firing positions.

Samuel could tell that some of the new recruits from Squad Ulanti had been killed, as they did not join the rest of the marines in the surge forward. Somewhere out there in the darkness were more marine corpses to tally against the value of the turbines, thought Samuel as he fired several rounds down at the mech-warrior.

For four years now, he had fought and killed for Grotto Corporation, and though he'd always known in the back of his head that all of his actions and decisions carried a certain monetary value, it never really hit home as hard as it did today. It was as if took the battle for the turbine station combined with the Errolite mercenary's recruitment speech to tear away the last scraps of the illusion he had been living.

His loyalty was not to Grotto and the Corporation's loyalty was not to him, it had always been about the money, for both sides. Only now was he seeing clearly that his relationship with Grotto was one-sided, even when it didn't have to be. He felt powerful in that moment, and it galvanized him to win this fight for himself, and Grotto could gnaw at the scraps.

The mech-warrior turned and spit rounds at his position after Samuel took a second potshot at the hostile war machine. Samuel held his hands on the ladder and his feet out to the sides so that he could control his rapid descent to the floor. His decision to move had been just in time, as the enemy's bullets tore a multitude of holes in the turbine and shredded much of the inner column. The mech-warrior's combat rifle might have seemed like a less than impressive weapon to have mounted on a war machine, but Samuel had to respect it more as he realized the rounds were armor piercing.

An explosion rocked the station as the plasma-lance burned through the heating coil of the turbine at Unit 17 and caused a series of secondary explosions. The marines were attacking the mech-warrior on all sides, and the Helion pilot was moving his machine in a continuous, even graceful, series of pirouettes as its mounted guns attempted to track the multitude of targets.

After a few moments of furious firefighting the mini-gun finally went dry and the plasma-lance sputtered through its final blast. In a matter of perhaps sixty seconds the marines had surrounded the mech-warrior.

Spencer emerged from the shadows with a "sticky" bomb and hurled it at the war machine. The bomb was a standard fragmentary grenade, as salvage marines were allowed no other type of explosive for fear that they would cause an unprofitable amount of collateral damage if allowed to have more incendiary devices. Spencer and a few of the other marines had started carrying sticks of a wax-like adhesive they used to coat their grenades to make them stick to whatever they were thrown against. The tactics did not work one hundred percent of the time and were not standard kit, but it worked enough that they kept doing it.

The pilot must have realized that he was about to be overrun and the mech-warrior's servo-legs groaned as he pushed the war machine into a sprint towards the exit.

Samuel had been approaching him from that side and realized as the mech-warrior turn towards him that Virginia was between them. Samuel raised his rifle and began pounding the mech's thick cockpit armor with concentrated fire as he got the pilot's attention. The war machine rushed past Virginia, who managed to fire a parting shot before hurling herself over the railing and into the shallow sump tank under the turbine.

Samuel turned to find cover as the mech-warrior opened up with its mounted combat rifle. His senses flared in pain as an armor piercing round drilled through his armor and struck him somewhere in the back. He instantly lost feeling from his chest down and collapsed in a heap. The force of the strike had spun him around and Samuel had landed on his back. He tried to raise his hand to reach for his gun, but found that he could not make it move. Before he could give too much thought to his unresponsive limbs, Spencer's sticky bomb exploded.

The frag grenade by itself would have not been enough to crack the mech's armor, but it had gotten stuck between a shoulder joint and what looked like the mech's empty ammunition canisters so the force of the blast did the real work. The mech's right arm was blown off, in addition to the ammunition canister, and the entire war-machine went crashing to the ground.

Samuel couldn't move his head, but from his vantage point he could see that the mech's pilot had been turned into something unrecognizable by the concussion of the blast inside the cockpit.

Samuel felt the darkness of unconsciousness start to slide over him, and he would have moved to inject himself with another stim hypo if he could only have moved his hands.

His mind wandered, moving from one moment in his life to the other, as if he was watching critical times in his life on playback, and he knew his life was coming to an end. In medic training they'd taught him about how the mind cycled through faded memories at the moment before expiration, as if searching for any last scrap of knowledge to aide in surviving.

Samuel found himself imagining his wife, standing before a beautiful house in a dark forest, the daydream they'd shared so many times since he became a Reaper. It was a pleasant fantasy, he thought as he felt himself finally slipping beneath the waves.

The gloom swallowed him and Samuel Hyst lay still as blood pooled underneath him.

UNTIL THAT DAY

A Note from the Author

Thank you for taking this grim adventure alongside the Reapers of Grotto Corporation. Though this was a hard end to a hard tale, this story is far from over. Forces align against one another in the depths of space and behind the closed doors of corporate boardrooms.

Stay alert for the next installment of the Necrospace series, where the journey will continue for some, and end for others at www.seanargo.wordpress.com

This is the job.

CHECK OUT OTHER GREAT SCIENCE FICTION BOOKS

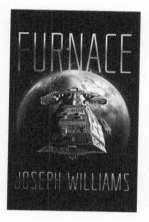

FURNACE
by Joseph Williams

On a routine escort mission to a human colony, Lieutenant Michael Chalmers is pulled out of hyper-sleep a month early. The RSA Rockne Hummel is well off course and—as the ship's navigator—it's up to him to figure out why. It's supposed to be a simple fix, but when he attempts to identify their position in the known universe, nothing registers on his scans. The vessel has catapulted beyond the reach of starlight by at least a hundred trillion light-years. Then a planetary-mass object materializes behind them. It's burning brightly even without a star to heat it. Hundreds of damaged ships are locked in its orbit. The crew discovers there are no life-signs aboard any of them. As system failures sweep through the Hummel, neither Chalmers nor the pilot can prevent the vessel from crashing into the surface near a mysterious ancient city. And that's where the real nightmare begins.

LUNA
by Rick Chesler

On the threshold of opening the moon to tourist excursions, a private space firm owned by a visionary billionaire takes a team of non-astronauts to the lunar surface. To address concerns that the moon's barren rock may not hold long-term allure for an uber-wealthy clientele, the company's charismatic owner reveals to the group the ultimate discovery: life on the moon.

But what is initially a triumphant and world-changing moment soon gives way to unrelenting terror as the team experiences firsthand that despite their technological prowess, the moon still holds many secrets.

CHECK OUT OTHER GREAT
SCIENCE FICTION BOOKS

IN PERPETUITY
by Jake Bible

For two thousand years, Earth and her many colonies across the galaxy have fought against the Estelian menace. Having faced overwhelming losses, the CSC has instituted the largest military draft ever, conscripting millions into the battle against the aliens. Major Bartram North has been tasked with the unenviable task of coordinating the military education of hundreds of thousands of recruits and turning them into troops ready to fight and die for the cause.

As Major North struggles to maintain a training pace that the CSC insists upon, he realizes something isn't right on the Perpetuity. But before he can investigate, the station dissolves into madness brought on by the physical booster known as pharma. Unfortunately for Major North, that is not the only nightmare he faces- an armada of Estelian warships is on the edge of the solar system and headed right for Earth!

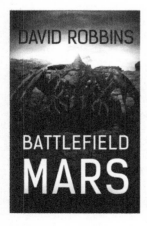

BATTLEFIELD MARS
by David Robbins

Several centuries into the future, Earth has established three colonies on Mars. No indigenous life has been discovered, and humankind looks forward to making the Red Planet their own.

Then 'something' emerges out of a long-extinct volcano and doesn't like what the humans are doing.

Captain Archard Rahn, United Nations Interplanetary Corps, tries to stem the rising tide of slaughter. But the Martians are more than they seem, and it isn't long before Mars erupts in all-out war.

CHECK OUT OTHER GREAT
SCIENCE FICTION BOOKS

MAUSOLEUM 2069
by Rick Jones

Political dignitaries including the President of the Federation gather for a ceremony onboard Mausoleum 2069. But when a cloud of interstellar dust passes through the galaxy and eclipses Earth, the tenants within the walls of Mausoleum 2069 are reborn and the undead begin to rise. As the struggle between life and death onboard the mausoleum develops, Eriq Wyman, a one-time member of a Special ops team called the Force Elite, is given the task to lead the President to the safety of Earth. But is Earth like Mausoleum 2069? A landscape of the living dead? Has the war of the Apocalypse finally begun? With so many questions there is only one certainty: in space there is nowhere to run and nowhere to hide.

RED CARBON
by D.J. Goodman

Diamonds have been discovered on Mars.

After years of neglect to space programs around the world, a ruthless corporation has made it to the Red Planet first, establishing their own mining operation with its own rules and laws, its own class system, and little oversight from Earth. Conditions are harsh, but its people have learned how to make the Martian colony home.

But something has gone catastrophically wrong on Earth. As the colony leaders try to cover it up, hacker Leah Hartnup is getting suspicious. Her boundless curiosity will lead her to a horrifying truth: they are cut off, possibly forever. There are no more supplies coming. There will be no more support. There is no more mission to accomplish. All that's left is one goal: survival.

 SEVERED**PRESS**

CHECK OUT OTHER GREAT SCIENCE FICTION BOOKS

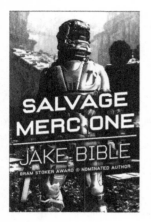

SALVAGE MERC ONE
by Jake Bible

Joseph Laribeau was born to be a Marine in the Galactic Fleet. He was born to fight the alien enemies known as the Skrang Alliance and travel the galaxy doing his duty as a Marine Sergeant. But when the War ended and Joe found himself medically discharged, the best job ever was over and he never thought he'd find his way again.

Then a beautiful alien walked into his life and offered him a chance at something even greater than the Fleet, a chance to serve with the Salvage Merc Corp.

Now known as Salvage Merc One Eighty-Four, Joe Laribeau is given the ultimate assignment by the SMC bosses. To his surprise it is neither a military nor a corporate salvage. Rather, Joe has to risk his life for one of his own. He has to find and bring back the legend that started the Corp.

SERENGETI
by J.B. Rockwell

It was supposed to be an easy job: find the Dark Star Revolution Starships, destroy them, and go home. But a booby-trapped vessel decimates the Meridian Alliance fleet, leaving Serengeti—a Valkyrie class warship with a sentient AI brain—on her own; wrecked and abandoned in an empty expanse of space. On the edge of total failure, Serengeti thinks only of her crew. She herds the survivors into a lifeboat, intending to sling them into space. But the escape pod sticks in her belly, locking the cryogenically frozen crew inside.

Then a scavenger ship arrives to pick Serengeti's bones clean. Her engines dead, her guns long silenced, Serengeti and her last two robots must find a way to fight the scavengers off and save the crew trapped inside her.